❧

BLUE DUST DAYS

❧

By
Laura McGrail

To the staff and students of

South Heights Elementary School,

a place where dreams come true.

Heart to Heart Publishing, Inc.
528 Mud Creek Road * Morgantown, KY 42261
(270) 526-5589
www.hearttoheartpublishinginc.com

Laura McGrail
Copyright ©2016
Publishing Rights: Heart to Heart Publishing, Inc.
Publishing Date February 14, 2017

Library of Congress Control No. 2016954458
ISBN_978-1-937008-48-2

Senior Editor: L.J. Gill
Editor: Susan J. Mitchell
Proof Reader: Nicki Bishop
Cover Illustration Jeanie Kittinger
Layout: Beth Walker

Printed in United States of America

First Edition
10 9 8 7 6 5 4 3 2

Heart to Heart Publishing, Inc. books are available at a special discount for bulk purchase in the US by corporations, institutions and other organizations. For more information, please contact Special Sales at (270) 526-5589

Chapter One

Freedom at last, I thought as I took a deep breath of clean, late winter air. Well, as clean as the air could be here in Whitburn, Kentucky, a mining town where a thin layer of coal dust settled on everything that didn't move. But we were lucky, Lem and me. Our family's house was the last in the row, halfway up the west hill looking down on the Clover Creek Mine. That meant we lived the farthest from the murky cloud that billowed forth every time the iron gates opened to take in or let out miners. It also meant that we had an actual patch of grass for playing ball.

"Come on, Lem, pitch him a good one," I shouted at my brother.

I had been cooped up for two long weeks, and I was anxious for my own turn at bat. But Lem, kindhearted as always, took his time to lob in a soft one so Timmy Crawford might actually hit the ball.

Timmy swung and missed again. "Strike seven, you're out!" I ran up to Timmy and took the bat out of his hands. "Your turn in the outfield."

Timmy nodded and trotted out to take my place. One good thing about Timmy; he always let us boss him around.

I turned to face my brother, twirling the bat. I took a couple practice swings, feeling the balance of the bat in my hands. Lem sure had made a good one this time. He found a bit of an ash tree and whittled it night after night until he had it to the perfect shape and weight. Then he rubbed it with axle grease until it shone. He had even carved his initials, L.S., and the year, 1933, into the handle.

Lem was smirking at me, and I knew that meant he was planning to throw a fastball outside. He thought he was good at keeping thoughts to himself, but I could read his face like the borrowed books I spent most of my spare time with. I closed my stance and hitched my hands a bit lower on the bat. Lem went into his windup and whizzed the ball at me.

Crack! I swung and hit the ball with all the power inside my eighty-five-pound body. The ball soared over Timmy's head, and he turned to race after it. I started to toss the bat away and run to the empty can we used for first base when I realized something was wrong.

I held only part of Lem's beloved bat in my hand. The other half lay on the grass. Lem rushed to my side and picked it up.

"Oh, Lem! I'm so sorry. I didn't mean to…"

A scream broke through my words. We looked toward the house and saw smoke pouring from the single window.

"The little ones!" I shouted and raced toward the back door.

I heard Lem yell at Timmy to run for help, and then his feet were pounding behind mine.

I yanked the door open, and a ball of black smoke came pouring out. "Down!" I yelled at Lem. "We have to get under the smoke."

The sitting room was dark as night as Lem and I crawled, feeling our way down the short hall to the small bedroom our parents shared with C.J. and Baby Emmie. Who would have thought that tiny hallway could seem so long as the seconds zoomed by? C.J. had gone quiet, and the eerie silence was more fearsome than his screams had been.

I heard Lem calling behind me in a voice he must have muffled with his shirt, "C.J.? Emmie? Where are you, sweethearts?"

I pulled my own sleeve away from my face to hush him. "Shush! I hear somethin'!" It was a low moan. I reached my hand out and felt a leg, then a waist, then an arm. I crawled next to Pap and put my face down close to his. "Pap, Pap! You've got to get up!"

My father grabbed my face between his two big hands. "Dessie? It can't happen again. It can't!"

I heard the anguish in his voice but had no idea what he was talking about, and I had no time to find out. I had caught the whiff of moonshine on his breath. I pushed him as best as I could back toward Lem.

"Get Pap out. I'll find the babies!"

As I crawled to where I thought the crib would be, I heard Lem pushing and pulling Pap's dead weight behind me. I found a skinny crib leg, covered my mouth with my shirt and pushed myself up. Frantically, I felt around the mattress until I found them, huddled together in a corner of the crib. I grabbed up one small form and held its mouth to my ear. It was Emmie. She was still breathing, thank the Lord! I tucked her in the crook of one arm and reached for C.J. His breathing was shallow, but he was still alive.

I clutched both small forms to my chest and headed back toward the main room. Tongues of fire reached toward us from across the room where the sofa was ablaze. I was so scared I thought my pounding heart was going to jump right out of my chest. With a combination of crawling and scooting, I was able to drag both little ones and myself to the back door. As I reached the open doorway, arms grabbed C.J. and Emmie from me. I flung myself out and drew great big breaths. Since the air was full of the same black smoke, I ended up coughing and spitting as I tried to clear my lungs.

Lem grabbed me and hugged me tight. "Dessie! I got Pap out, with the help of Mr. Crawford."

I pulled away and looked at my brother's face. Lem was two and a half years older than me, but he was small for his age, and we were the same height. Besides, as far back as I could remember, I had been the leader between us. Lem was the kindest, gentlest person in Whitburn. It was me who had gotten him into scrapes over the years and Lem who had gotten us out of them because he had a magic way with adults. They looked at his blond hair, blue eyes and sweet smile and forgave Lem of anything. I got included as sort of a package deal.

Now black blotches ran through his blond hair and soot covered his thin cheeks. I guessed I looked the same. "The babies! Where are they?"

He turned me around and pointed. "They're okay, too. Mam and Miz Crawford have them."

I pushed past the volunteer fire brigade passing buckets of water hand to hand. Mam was seated on the bench under the blue ash tree with two-year-old C.J. on her lap. Our neighbor was holding Emmie, bouncing her up and down to calm her. Mam crooned, "Oh my babies, oh my babies," as she rocked C.J. back and forth in her arms.

I felt my heart start up again at the sight of my baby brother and sister, both of them squirming and squalling. They were sooty and their faces were streaked with tears, but I saw no other signs of the fire on them.

Mam looked up at us, tears streaming down her careworn face. "Dessie. Lem. You saved them, didn't you? You saved our little ones." She held out one hand, and I knelt and grabbed it while Lem put an arm around her shoulders. She looked up with the special smile she always reserved just for him. For once, I didn't even feel the usual pang of jealousy.

We watched the men of the town carry out the charred remains of the sofa and the big chair Pap always sat in. *Pap*! I hadn't even spared one moment of thought for him. I sighed and guessed I should.

As I opened my mouth to ask, Pap appeared out of the hazy air around us. His huge frame blocked my view of the house. One arm was held in a makeshift sling.

He rushed to Mam and pushed me out of the way without noticing. Pap stroked C.J.'s head gently as he and Mam looked long into each other's eyes. Then he reached out and patted Emmie's back gently too. I stood there staring. It had been such a long time since I'd seen Pap be gentle. These days he was mostly angry, drunk, or passed out.

Pap looked around like he'd just realized there were people in the yard watching. He opened his arm wide and tried to hug us all, including Miz Crawford.

"Oh my family, my family," his big voice boomed. "The Lord has seen fit to spare us. Let us pray together and thank the Almighty." Miz Crawford reached for C.J. and ducked out of the family circle, her nose wrinkling daintily at the scent of moonshine coming off Pap.

"Lil, I'll take the babies to my house tonight. I'll see they get fed and sleep well." Mam smiled her thanks and waved at C.J., who was looking back over Miz Crawford's shoulder.

Lem and Mam ignored the alcohol smell and bowed their heads, but Pap's words made me angrier than a pissed-off hornet, and I forgot for a moment the family code of silence.

"The Lord had nothin' to do with it. Lem and me got the babies out, and you too. Although why we bothered with you, I don't know, since it was your drinkin' and smokin' that caused this!"

Pap noticed me now, and his face turned white with fury under the black streaks and smudges. He drew his good arm back to slap me but remembered we had an audience. He grabbed me instead and pressed me against his chest in a crushing hug. "Now, now, my girl. It's all right. No need to go into female hysterics. Your pa'll take care of everything."

Well, that's what he said out loud. What he whispered to me was, "Hush your mouth if you want to be able to sit down tomorrow."

I got the message. I sank to my knees when he released me and bowed my head while Pap prayed long and loud until Gordon Johnson walked over.

"Calton, we're through here, and the boys are going home to supper. Most of your belongings were saved, but they're full of smoke and the house is a total loss. I'm sorry, but your lot is going to have to find another place to stay. Mr. Hampton is on his way up."

Pap thumped Mr. Johnson on the back with his good hand. "Sorry I wasn't much use to you fellows, with this bum arm and all. Give my thanks to the boys, Gordon. The family will be fine. I know Joe Hampton will come through for us."

I looked at Lem and rolled my eyes. Pap was good at pouring on the charm, but we knew the other side of his personality. I had just finished two weeks of being his nursemaid while he was laid up with a hurt leg. Pap was on the day shift at the mine. Two weeks ago, he had fallen in a shaft and landed on his pickaxe. At least that was the story he put about. I had my suspicions, but I only shared them with Lem. Anyhow, Pap was off work, which meant that I had to miss school to watch the little ones and wait on Pap while Mam cleaned house at the Hamptons'.

Every morning after Mam left home and Pap was still snoring away, I searched all the hiding places I could think of for the moonshine his pal Lester supplied him with. If I found it, I poured it out and tossed the jars or bottles. But most every afternoon, I'd find him half drunk and have to sober him up with black coffee before Mam came home. Today, he had seemed sober. His leg was healed, and he was supposed to return to work tomorrow. When Lem asked if I could have a break and play ball, Pap ruffled his hair and shooed us out, saying he'd watch C.J. and Emmie. I swear we had only been playing for a few minutes. The man could get drunk faster than a racehorse could run! And now he had a bum arm? I couldn't stand two more weeks of taking care of him, plus I missed school. I especially loved grammar class and my teacher, Miss Morrissey.

These thoughts swirled through my brain as I watched the fire brigade break apart and nod to the gray-haired, well-dressed man walking slowly up the hill toward our house. Mr. James Joseph Hampton was manager of the Clover Creek Mine, one of dozens of coal mines owned by his family's business, Unified Steel. He was a nephew to the J.J. Hampton who owned the company, but even so, *family* was a big theme with Mr. Hampton. He liked to say how the mine workers, their wives and their children were all part of his family and that he was the head of the family and took care of all of us. Well, if you call paying low wages for dangerous, backbreaking work that makes young men old taking care of us, he did that right well. He took such good care of us that nobody could leave, unless Mr. Joe fired him, because we all needed to live in the row houses the mine owned and buy from the company store.

Mr. Joe and his wife lived in a big house on the hill on the other side of town, away from the mine smoke and soot. His snooty wife thought Mam had refinement and let her come clean their house whenever Pap had been on a bender and couldn't work for a while.

Mr. Joe and his sidekick, Harlow Gumbs, picked their way through the debris in our yard. The small crowd of women and children who had been looking on during the excitement of the fire melted away at the arrival of the boss man. Mr. Joe handed his silver-topped walking stick to the stout Mr. Gumbs, nodded at Mam and took the dainty handkerchief away from his mouth to speak to Pap.

"Hello, Calton. This is a sad sight, indeed."

"Yes, indeed," echoed Mr. Gumbs.

"But a day of miracles, wouldn't you say, Mr. Joe?" boomed Pap. "My entire family was spared."

"Ah yes, that is quite a miracle."

"Certainly, certainly," said Mr. Gumbs.

"Tell me, please, however did this fire start?"

Pap didn't pause for a moment. I realized he'd already been getting the story straight in his own head. "Why, Mr. Joe, it was a pure accident, it was. My girl here," he pushed me forward, "she went outside for a moment and got distracted, I figure, playing baseball. The beans spilled over on the stove and caught on fire. I was watchin' the little ones while Lil was at your house. I crawled through the fire and smoke to get the babies out of the house. I busted my arm when a beam fell on us and I shielded them."

"It appears you are a hero then."

Pap looked pleased, while I seethed inside. Mr. Joe wasn't finished with Pap though.

"However, this is an additional loss to our mining family, Calton. A loss of revenue, you understand. The mine cannot sustain such losses, especially when the country is in the midst of a depression. First, with your, uhm, injury, we have the loss of your services for another week or so, and second, we have the loss of a home that belongs to the mine. Someone has to pay for these losses. What should we do about this, do you think?"

"Yes, what?" asked Mr. Gumbs.

Pap had the decency to look ashamed but only for a moment. "My boy will work for me, Mr. Joe. Lemuel is small for his age, but he's goin' on sixteen, and that's plenty old enough to go in the mine. He can work my shifts until my arm is whole again."

Mr. Hampton ignored the gasps from three of Pap's family members. He nodded his head slowly as he studied Lem through slitted eyes. "He is a small one. Alright, he can go in the mine, but only at half-pay. He can't mine as much coal in a day as you can. But he'll continue to work after you return too. His wages will go toward the repayment of the house."

My hands balled into fists at my sides while Lem looked stunned and Mam began to cry softly. Mr. Hampton chose to take her tears as a sign of gratitude. He snapped his fingers at Mr. Gumbs.

"Harlow has the key to number five. As you know, it's been vacant since Tom Tippen's unfortunate accident. Now, now, Mrs. Soames, did you think Joe Hampton would let you and yours be out in the cold tonight? Of course not. You are welcome, I'm sure. Just sign the usual renters' agreement, and you can move in." He put his finger under Lem's chin and tipped it up. "You, young man, are starting an exciting new life with Clover Creek Mine. I will tell the shift boss, Mr. McGuire, to expect you tomorrow at 5:00 a.m. sharp."

Joe Hampton's lips parted in what I guess was the closest he could come to a smile as he held out his hand to Mr. Gumbs for his walking stick. "Good evening, all. No need to assist me, I'm sure." He turned and began walking carefully through the clothes and furniture scattered in the yard.

Mr. Gumbs shoved a grimy piece of paper and a pen at my father. Pap made his mark on the line Mr. Gumbs pointed to. The assistant handed the key of our new house to Pap, nodded his head toward Mam and then hurried after the retreating figure of the mine boss.

Three shocked faces turned to Pap.

Chapter Two

Pap went on the defensive really quick. "Now don't you go lookin' at me like that. If I hadn't suggested Lem for the mine, Mr. Joe would have said it anyhow. I was tryin' to work it out so the boy could just work temporary."

"Well, temporary isn't what Mr. Joe said!" I spat the words at Pap.

"Listen here, girl. I've had about all I can take from you." He shook his fist in my direction, but I was beyond caring. Lem couldn't go in the mine, he just couldn't!

Pap appealed to Mam. "Besides, Lil, we knew this day would come. We've just been puttin' it off because you're soft on him." He jerked his head toward Lem, who stood still as a statue, his eyes flicking from face to face. "There's no future in Whitburn for any man except the mine. We all know that."

Lem suddenly came to life. He stood on his tiptoes and put his face close to Pap's. His voice was low but clear and controlled. "I'll go in the mine. I'll do it for Mam and Dessie, for C.J. and Emmie. But I won't be doin' it for you. And as soon as I can, I'll be out from under your roof. I

may have to be a miner, but I don't have to be a man like you, and I

never will be."

Lem turned away and stalked off. I started to run after him, but Mam

put a hand on my arm. "Leave him be, Dess. He needs some time to

himself. Besides, I could use your help."

I looked at my mother and thought how alike she and Lem were—alike

on the outside and the inside. They shared the same blue eyes and blond

hair, but more importantly, they were kind and gentle, patient and

forgiving. Unlike Pap and me. I didn't like to admit it, but in addition to

sharing his dark eyes and curly brown hair, I shared other traits. Like

him, I was quick to anger and slow to forgive. Well, the anger building in

me was just starting to simmer.

In our quiet moments, I had talked many times with Mam about Lem's

future and how we wanted him away from Whitburn one day. We knew

he was too frail to breathe in black dust for years to come. We knew he

had bigger dreams than this tiny town, too. Funny thing, though. Mam

never asked me about my dreams for my future.

Now she looked intently in my eyes, and I guessed she was thinking

the same things about Lem but also silently begging me to leave it alone with Pap. I nodded to her and started sorting through the smoky, damp piles the fire had left behind.

I helped Mam sort and pack our meager belongings. Our clothes and bedding would have to be washed and aired out before we could use them again. The pots and pans, oil lamps and dishes we packed up to take to the new place. Mr. Hampton provided furniture, such as it was, in all the company houses. So we'd have beds to sleep in, but there would be no blankets to ward off the chill of the night air for a while.

I looked over at the twisted wood and metal that had been the icebox. The heat of the fire had melted the big block of ice and the metal brackets and bolts. None of the food that had been in the icebox was worth saving, and the bits and pieces that had been in the cupboards were ruined too. My stomach grumbled, and I coughed to hide the sound. Mam didn't need to add me being hungry to her long list of worries.

Pap rummaged aimlessly among the charred remains. I figured he was looking for a bottle, but he surprised me by holding up the small wooden chest I knew they always kept in their bedroom. Now blackened around the edges, it had been a pretty thing with carvings of flowers and leaves. I liked to run my hand over its smoothly varnished lid whenever I dusted in their room. But the chest also had a brass lock, and I had never before seen what was in it. Pap fished a key from a chain around his neck and twisted the lock open.

"I found them, Lil! They're still safe." His face glowed with pleasure.

I craned my neck to see what was in the box, but all I caught was a gleam of gold amid some papers.

"I'm so glad, Calton," said my mother quietly. "I know how important your medals and certificates are to you. It would have been awful to have lost them."

Medals and certificates? I wanted to puke. I wanted to scream and beat him up. Here we were, trying to recover what we could of the mess Pap had made, and he was worried about some worthless trinkets! I had hoped Pap had a secret money stash in that box. I loved my mother, but I did not understand her letting him get by with treating us so badly. Of course, that was nothing new; this had been the pattern of our lives for as long as I could remember. Standing there surrounded by charred furniture, burned-up toys and smoke-filled clothes, I vowed that I would never forgive Pap for all the misery he had caused today.

I needed to get away from him. "Mam, can I go on over to the new house and take a load of this stuff?"

I think Mam suspected what I was feeling. "Calton, if you'll give me the key to number five, Dessie and I will get started moving in. Perhaps you can see what shape Emmie's high chair and the babies' crib is in. We need to salvage whatever we can. We're out of scrip, so I guess we'll have to pay on account to replace some of our lost things."

Pap was still rummaging through his box and didn't seem to hear the despair in Mam's voice. He absentmindedly handed the key over. "I'll bring them over in a little while."

I loaded up Timmy's loaned wagon, and Mam filled her arms as best she could. My heart sank to realize we could get most of our belongings moved in one trip. We walked slowly down the dirt track that served as the street between the two rows of houses. It didn't take us long to get from number twenty to number five.

All the houses were the same; only from the numbers could you tell them apart. Each house was square, flat-roofed and covered in gray clapboard that once was white. Mr. Hampton never had the houses repainted since there was no use in it. Anything white turned to gray soon enough thanks to the coal dust. Each was the same inside too—one middle room that served as parlor and dining room, one small kitchen off the back and one small bedroom on each side of the middle room. Since our family was one of the smaller ones, I shared a bedroom only with Lem. I guessed Mam and Pap would be moving C.J. in with us once he outgrew the crib.

An outhouse and a pump were shared by every two houses. It was my job to pump and haul water in every day for cooking, cleaning and washing dishes. Every Saturday afternoon, I hauled in extra buckets. Mam would heat the water on the stove and pour it into the tin bathtub, and we'd all take turns taking baths in the kitchen.

Mam would sigh and remember how she would take a bath every day growing up. I didn't know much more than that about Mam's family. She wouldn't talk about them and only hinted at some trouble that had happened before any of us kids were born. She just said that she and Pap weren't welcome at her parents' home anymore. Sometimes I would dream about going there. In my dreams, my grandparents lived in a big red brick house with ivy growing up the side and a wide porch on the front. They opened the door and welcomed me in, hugging me tightly and telling me I was wonderful. Then my tall and jolly grandfather carried me up a wide flight of stairs and dumped me in a bathtub of my own. We laughed and laughed at my wet clothes and shoes.

"Why, that's strange. The door is unlocked," said Mam, breaking into my daydream. She pushed the door open and gasped in delight. I hurried in behind her.

A pair of faded sheets hung over the window as makeshift curtains. A fire was burning in the coal stove in the middle room, and the table was covered with a cheerful red and white tablecloth. It was set for four with mismatched plates and cups and a lighted oil lamp. The delicious smell of fresh bread baking wafted through the house.

"Ah, you're here. Come in, come in, my dears," said Verna Gumbs. As much as the mining families of Whitburn detested Harlow Gumbs, they adored his wife. Miz Gumbs was also short and stout, but as much as Harlow was mean and miserly, his wife was friendly and generous. The Gumbses had no children of their own, but Mother Gumbs, as we all called her, was unofficial grandmother to all the town's children.

Mother Gumbs swallowed Mam in a hug. "There, there, now. You've had an awful day, Lillian dear." She shot a sympathetic look my way. "You too, Dessie. Thank the Lord you were all spared. Lil, sit here by the stove, and I'll bring you a nice cup of chamomile tea while Dessie and I unpack. When the menfolk arrive, I'll serve up the stew and sourdough bread. And Minnie Perkins brought over an apple pie."

"Oh, Verna, my children won't go hungry tonight. How can I ever thank you?" asked Mam gratefully. Tears slid down her face. It seemed strange to me that she didn't cry about the fire but now she was crying about the ladies' kindness. Adults were so confusing sometimes.

"Hush now, honey. I know you'd do the same for me and mine if ever we were in need. All the ladies, excepting mean old Thelma Pike and Miz Hampton, of course, have been in and out of this house today, soon as I saw Harlow take a key to number five. We dusted away the cobwebs and made up the beds and gathered odds and ends of food. There may be a Depression on, but like Mr. Joe says, we are one big family."

As she talked, Mother Gumbs bustled around, fixing tea for Mam and covering her with a coverlet that I knew she had knitted herself. She was famous for her knitting. Every newborn baby in Whitburn received booties and a cap from Mother Gumbs, and every new bride was given a knitted blanket or coverlet. I was relieved to see Mam lean back in the one soft chair in the house with a contented sigh and close her eyes. I hoped Pap wouldn't be in a hurry to show up after all, but I was worried about Lem.

I carried in the things from the wagon and put them away where Mother Gumbs directed. That small chore only took a few minutes. Then she pushed me in the direction of the kitchen, where she had a sink of warm water waiting with a rough towel and a bar of lye soap. I realized that the pervasive smell of smoke was coming off me as I scrubbed my arms, legs and face. Mother Gumbs helped me wash my hair and towel it half-dry and re-braid it. I wasn't used to having someone help me, but it was a real comforting feeling.

"Don't you look like your lovely self again?" asked Mother Gumbs as she helped me change into borrowed clothes. I hugged her in grateful surprise. Nobody had ever called me lovely before. I wondered if this must be what it was like to really have a grandmother.

"These clothes are from Lizzie Barnes next door. They're a bit big, but I can fix that." Mother Gumbs pulled a safety pin from her pocket and twisted my shirt until she was satisfied. While she was working on my clothes, I thought how there was one good thing with the move to number five. Lizzie was the one girl at school I liked. It might be nice to have a friend nearby.

After my quick half-bath, I went to empty what was left in Timmy's wagon. The last were the bits and pieces that Lem and I cherished. I had retrieved them from our room at number twenty and took them into our new bedroom. I laid them out on the small dresser. There was Lem's baseball, his lucky horseshoe and his rock collection. Next to those, I placed the 1928 World's Fair postcard Sally Johnson had sent me and the braided reed bracelet Lem had made. Both now smelled faintly of smoke. I thumbed through my most prized possession, a secondhand edition of *Little Women* that Mam had given me for Christmas two years before. It was the only book we owned, and I had read it a dozen times. The fire had touched it a bit, blackening the edges of some of the pages, but I could still read every word. I hugged it to my chest in thankfulness.

I looked around the tiny bedroom and noticed that the twin beds were covered in hand-knitted blankets from Mother Gumbs. She must have a stockpile of knitted pieces in the house she shared with Harlow. I grinned at the thought of him surrounded by baby booties and doilies.

My happier mood was shattered by the slamming of the door. I hurried to the main room. Pap dragged in the crib and high chair. They reeked of smoke but looked sound. After offering Verna Gumbs a hearty greeting, he carried his precious wooden box and the crib to the other bedroom. I decided it was time to find Lem.

"Mam, I think I know where Lem might be. I'll go and bring him home."

"Yes, do that. It's getting dark. I'll hold some supper for you both."

I hugged Mother Gumbs again and whispered thank you and then turned toward the door.

"And Dessie," Mam said quietly. "Tell Lem not to fret. You and I will think of a way to get him out of the mine."

Chapter Three

I left the house and turned down the road. It was officially named Evelyn Way after Miz Hampton, but we all called it Rowhouse Road Two. Whitburn was laid out in a rough V pattern across the two hills and valley of our holler. Two roads of mine-owned houses clung to the sides of the western hill. In the valley lay the Clover Creek Mine entrance and the railroad line where the five-ton coal cars rumbled back and forth all hours of the day. Here, too, were other mine buildings—offices for the manager, the paymaster, and the clerks; miners' washrooms; and the company store where the mining families did their shopping since part of each miner's pay was given in scrip that could only be used at the mine's store. The company store was the center of social life in Whitburn.

Every Saturday morning, Mam would drag me with her, and I'd look at things we had no money to buy while Mam visited with the other ladies who were shopping. Mam would agonize over each purchase of food, oil, clothing and fabric as she tried to make Pap's weekly scrip allotment stretch as far as possible. Mam was good at making a penny go a far piece. Each year, she planted a garden and canned vegetables that we ate all winter long. She never spent money on herself but spent many an hour sewing clothes for us kids or piecing scraps of fabric into beautiful quilts. Her favorite pastime was getting together with other women for a quilting bee, where they all stitched on a quilt while they gossiped about whatever lady wasn't there that evening.

As I walked along, I thought about all the times Mam had tried to get me to stitch a straight row. Every time ended up with both of us frustrated. I was grateful whenever I lay warm and contented under one of Mam's quilts, but I just didn't have the patience to stitch. I sighed as I realized that the fire had probably ruined all the quilts. Maybe I would try again to sew and help her make new ones. If Lem had to work in the mine, I guess I could sit and sew, even though I'd hate it.

The mine entrance was closed and quiet. The next shift wouldn't be starting for another hour. As I passed it, I gazed upward to the right of the full moon, and there it was: my star, my wishing star. Tonight I didn't wish the wishes I usually wished: that we would no longer be poor or that we could have meat more than twice a week. I closed my eyes and wished with all my might that I could find a way to keep Lem out of the mine.

I climbed slowly up the main road along the eastern hill where the school, the few shops in town and a handful of nicer houses where the shop owners lived were located. The street was quiet since most folks were home to their suppers. I nodded to Mr. Thomas, the barber, as he was locking up. I walked past Doc Larkins's office and the dentist's office next door. I cut across the yard of Whitburn Public School. I noticed a light on in Miss Morrissey's classroom and wondered if she had missed me the past two weeks, but I didn't have time to stop. She was the teacher for junior high and early high school grades, so Lem was in my class, but next year, he'd be moving up to Miz Cantrell's upper high school class. If we found a way for him to stay in school, that is. I sighed and hurried up Lincoln Drive toward the gray stone house that looked down on the town. This was where Joe and Evelyn Hampton lived.

My destination was not the big house. Before I reached the Hamptons' flagstone driveway, I veered right and headed up a small dirt track toward a field they owned. It was dark among the trees, and I shivered as the evening's chill hit my bare legs sticking out below my dress. I knew Lem wouldn't be shivering. He never seemed to feel the cold, and even in the dead of winter, he would wander the hillsides for hours on end. He loved to pick berries, look for colorful rocks to add to his collection, or track animals just to watch them. Whenever we both finished our chores early, Lem would let me tag along. He wasn't as good a student at school as I was, but he knew the names of all the trees and plants and animals around our small town.

He was particular to animals and was forever bringing strays home. Lem would find hurt or abandoned animals in the woods, like birds, squirrels and, one memorable time, a baby raccoon, and beg to keep them. Pap would yell and Mam would sigh about the bother, but they always gave in. Hardly anybody could resist saying yes to Lem. He was so easygoing and goodhearted. He never asked for anything for himself. He spent every free minute tending to the wounded animal and then released it back into the woods when it could fend for itself. He got kind of a reputation as an animal healer, and folks started bringing animals to him, since there was no regular veterinarian in town.

That's how he got to know Miz Hampton. Evelyn Hampton's only interest in life was her horses. Folks said Evelyn Hampton poured all her love into her horses and had none left over for anybody else, including Mr. Joe. She kept a stable of a dozen or so, and it was rumored that the Hamptons bet heavily on races when they traveled.

About a year ago, Mr. Gumbs pounded on our door in the middle of the night and demanded that Lem come with him to the Hamptons'. Pap had gone along too. Lem told me all about it the next day. Mr. Gumbs led Pap and Lem to the stables behind the Hamptons' house. Miz Evelyn sat cradling the head of a mare in her lap. The mare was in labor, but the foal was breach, and they were both going to die if the foal couldn't be turned. Mr. Gumbs and several of the other hands working for the Hamptons had tried, but their arms were too big. Miz Evelyn asked Lem to save the foal and its mama, who was her dear, dear Sadie.

Pap nodded yes and soaped Lem's arm so it was all slippery, and then Lem reached in clear up to his armpit. After much tugging, he was able to turn that foal around in its mother's womb. Next thing you knew, the foal slid right out and was soon standing on its own, drinking milk and being nuzzled by Sadie. Anyhow, Miz Evelyn was beside herself with joy. She hugged Lem and thanked him over and over. Pap told Lem to ask her for money, but he wouldn't do it. He told me that saving that foal had been the best thing he'd ever done. I smiled now at the memory of the wonder on Lem's face as he said that.

As they were leaving, Miz Evelyn asked Lem if there was anything he wanted. He asked her if he could ride the older horses in the meadow sometime. She told him he could anytime, and last summer, she had even let him ride one of her horses in the county fair race. On his first try out, Lem had won, beating grown men who had been racing for years. People said they'd never seen such a natural-born rider as my brother.

That's how I knew where Lem would be today. He came to visit the horses whenever he could. It flitted through my mind that maybe we could ask Miz Evelyn to talk to Mr. Joe about Lem staying out of the mine. Maybe she could make him her horse-doctor-in-training or something.

A few more steps and I emerged into a small clearing. There he was, leaning against the black wooden fence, his blond hair shining in the moonlight.

Lem didn't turn around when he spoke.

"You didn't have to come fetch me. I know where number five is."

"I was worried about you."

Lem put an arm around my shoulder when I came up to him. "I'll be okay. I knew I'd end up in the mine one day. I just wish I'd had a bit of warnin', you know? I don't even get to tell the fellas at school, and I would have liked to say goodbye to Miss Morrissey."

"I'll tell her for you. But Lem, we'll figure out a way for you to quit the mine when Pap goes back to work. I don't care what Mr. Joe said. You'll just go work for Pap for a couple weeks, that's all."

"That won't happen, Dess. Once a fella starts in the mine, he can't stop. Mr. Hampton won't let me. Pap won't let me."

Lem sighed. "I'm not really afraid, not of dyin' anyway. That comes up top to folks just like it does down below. I just don't know if I can stand bein' cooped up for years and years. You remember last year…"

"Sure I do," I said. We stood in silence, each of us remembering.

Work at Clover Creek, like all eastern Kentucky coal mines during the Depression, could be irregular. Whenever the stockpiled coal amount was greater than what the company needed, Mr. Gumbs would post a sign saying No Work Tomorrow on the main gate. Sometimes that sign would stay up for days. The first day, Pap would laugh and say he was on holiday, but if the days dragged on, he got short-tempered, and we all knew he was worrying about the bills, since the mining families still had to buy food and pay the mine company for rent even on days when the miners didn't work.

The summer before, there'd been a spell of six days with no work for the men. Midweek, Pap got tired of finding us underfoot and released us from our chores. We headed to Taylor's Pond, a favorite swimming hole among our classmates. Lem peeled off his shirt, grabbed the rope hanging from a tree and swung out over the pond. He let go and splashed mightily, landing between Bobby Wilcox and Tony Phelps, who promptly dunked him when he surfaced. I dived into the pond and swam laps until my arms ached, relishing the feel of the cool water on my hot skin. After my swim, I joined Linda Sue Barnett and Jenny McIntyre, who were sunning themselves on shore.

"Dessie, stop drippin' on me!" griped Jenny. I moved closer to Linda Sue.

"Now you're throwin' a shadow on my legs," Linda Sue complained.

"Oh don't make such a hoo-ha," I said and sat down on a large tree root sticking out of the ground. "All you girls want to do anymore is sit around posin' for the boys. I've got news for you. They aren't even lookin' this way."

Linda Sue stopped fluffing her new hairdo in mid-fluff to peek at the boys goofing off in the water. "You're impossible, Dessie," she fussed and raised her voice to call, "Oh Bobby?"

"What do you want, Linda Sue?"

She gave him a pout. "We're bored. Can't you boys come out and think of somethin' else we could do?" Bobby hesitated, and she added, "You're so smart. I bet you know a place we've never been before."

Bobby shrugged to the fellows and waded to shore, followed by Tony and Lem. My brother sat down on the tree root while the other boys lounged on the grass.

"I do know of a place we could explore," said Bobby. "The mine." I felt Lem stiffen next to me.

Tony laughed. "The mine's closed. We can't get in."

"I know of another way in that my pa showed me once."

"Why would we want to go in that dirty place?" asked Jenny.

Linda Sue nudged Jenny. "That dark place you mean." She stared at Jenny until her friend's eyes widened and she nodded. The boys seemed clueless, but I knew what those looks meant.

I stood up. "Let's go home, Lem."

"Yeah, Lem. Do what your little sister says, like always," said Tony, and the girls laughed.

"Come on. Don't be a scaredy-cat." Bobby stood and held out a hand. Lem hesitated but then took it, and Bobby hauled him to his feet. The others started gathering their belongings and pulling shirts and cotton dresses on over their wet bathing clothes.

I drew Lem aside. "I know you don't want to do this."

He pulled away from me. "Leave me be, Dess. I'm goin' with the fellas. Why don't you run on home?"

I stuck out my jaw stubbornly. "If you're goin', I'm goin'."

We followed Bobby along a stream that wound through the hills around the mine. Halfway up Knob Hill, he turned and ducked into a stand of pine trees. He pulled aside some low-hanging branches to reveal an opening in the hill surrounded by rough wooden planks.

"You sure this is safe, Bobby?" I asked.

He nodded. "Sure I'm sure. Besides, we won't go far down the tunnel. Here, Tony, I've got one candle; you take the other."

Bobby went forward through the doorway, and Linda Sue quickly ducked in after him. Tony and Jenny were next, with Lem and me bringing up the rear. Through the light of the flickering candles ahead, I could see Linda Sue clutching Bobby's free arm, while Jenny held Tony's hand tightly. I made a sound of disgust, but neither girl looked back.

The tunnel was narrow with a low ceiling. Even I had to hunch down a bit as we walked. Darker holes indicating smaller tunnels led off from the one we were taking, and I thought that if anyone ever got lost in the mine, they might be lost for good.

Just as I was thinking this, Bobby snapped his fingers, and the lights ahead flickered off. We were engulfed in total darkness. A girl screamed up ahead, and I heard Lem gasp behind me. At first I couldn't do anything but deal with my own reaction. I put my hand in front of my eyes and couldn't see it at all. I suddenly noticed the damp in the air and a cold breeze blowing. The darkness seemed like something alive. I felt it growing around me, pushing in and squeezing the breath out of me. I shook my head to get rid of these thoughts and reached out for Lem but couldn't find him. I shouted his name, but he didn't answer. My heartbeat quickened.

One boy shouted and the other cursed, but Jenny would not quit screaming. I couldn't get them to listen to me while Jenny was yelling. I think Tony finally put a hand over Jenny's mouth because she shut up all of a sudden. A light flickered on as Bobby relit his candle.

"Bobby, Lem's missing!"

"What do you mean?" he demanded.

I explained what had happened when the lights went out.

Bobby sighed heavily. "Maybe he went back outside. Follow me."

We traipsed back the way we had come, but when we stepped outside, there was no sign of Lem. We all called, but he didn't answer. I turned to Bobby.

"He's still inside. We have to find him, now!"

Bobby nodded. "You girls stay here. Tony and I will go look for him."

"I want to go, too."

Bobby leaned close and spoke in a low voice. "Look, Dessie, we only have two candles. It'll be faster if Tony and I go alone. Besides, if we aren't back in an hour, you'll have to get help. Do you think either of those dumb clucks will remember the way back to town?" He jerked a thumb at Linda Sue and Jenny and I giggled, despite my fear for Lem.

"Okay, but if you don't bring him out, I'll tell the girls how you planned that trick back there to scare them." He lifted an eyebrow in surprise but didn't deny my accusation.

I sat in the sun near the mine entrance for over an hour. Linda Sue and Jenny sprawled in the shade, offering a steady stream of complaints. After a few minutes, I tuned them out and instead imagined a thousand different ways that Lem could have hurt himself or died in the mine.

Just when I had decided I needed to go for help, I heard the boys coming back toward the entrance. Bobby came first, followed by Lem, with Tony last. I was so glad to see Lem that I pushed past Bobby to give my brother a hug.

"Lem! I was afraid you were lost for good," I blubbered.

He pulled away, embarrassed. "I'm fine, Dess."

Linda Sue got to her feet and stepped over to us. "So what happened, Lemmy?" she asked in an annoying, fake-nice voice. "Did the wittle boy get wost?"

"Leave him alone," demanded Jenny. "Anybody with any sense would have been scared in that dark hole. Come on, Lem." She took him by the arm and turned toward the stream and the way back to town.

"Do you have to act like an idiot, or is it not an act?" Bobby growled at Linda Sue as he passed her.

"What did I do? Bobby? Bobby!" She rushed on, leaving Tony shaking his head in confusion.

"Come on, Tony. You're stuck with me, I guess." He shrugged, and we headed after the other four.

By suppertime, the whole town knew. We found out the story had spread when Pap stormed into the house. He had been lounging on the store's porch when Harlow Gumbs came up and escorted him to Mr. Joe's office, where he found the fathers of Bobby, Tony, Linda Sue and Jenny already waiting.

"Mr. Joe told us he'd learned that our children had entered the mine illegally and asked if we needed more time off work to get better control of our households. Then he docked us each a dollar for the cost of boardin' up that old entrance." Pap glared at us.

"We'll pay back the dollar, Pap," I said, but he ignored me.

"Guess what happened next," he went on. "Mr. Joe asked me to stay after the others left, and I had to hear how my son got lost and had to be rescued." He shook his finger in Lem's face. "No son of mine is a coward!"

Pap gave Lem the worst whipping he'd ever had. When I told Pap that Lem couldn't help being scared, Pap turned around and gave me a couple of licks too. Then he stomped off to Lester's.

Lem told me his side of the story at bedtime. When the lights went out, he reacted without thinking. He took off blindly, heading back toward the entrance. The panic I had felt must have been about a hundred times as bad for him. He'd never been as scared in his whole life, and he'd felt like he was being swallowed alive in the dusty blackness. Anyhow, he must have taken a wrong turn, and that led to another wrong turn until he was totally lost. Lem wandered and yelled for help but then decided he should sit down and hope for rescue. Lem thanked Bobby after he found him and apologized over and over, but their friendship hadn't been the same since.

"You swore that night you'd never go down in the mine again, Lem."

"I was wrong to say that. I was just angry, and my rear was sore."

I reached out and hugged him around the waist. "If you could choose, what would you do instead someday?"

Lem smiled at me, and his whole face lit up. "I'd ride horses. I'd be a jockey and race at Churchill Downs." He sighed. "Oh, Dess, if I could do that, I could maybe make enough money to take the whole family out of Whitburn for good. Just imagine it."

I caught his mood. "You'd wear yellow and purple silks, and you'd win the Derby and be famous. And we'd live in a red brick house with white shutters and a huge porch."

"Yeah, and the windows would look out on acres of green grass with not a speck of coal dust anywhere."

"And we'd eat bacon every day of the week and twice on Sunday!"

"Oh, Dessie," laughed Lem. "Your daydreams always end in bacon." He laughed so hard he doubled over, and when he straightened up, he had tears running down his face.

"I can dream bigger than that, you know," I pouted.

"Okay. Tell me a big dream. What would you do if you could choose?"

I leaned on the wooden fence and looked up at the moon. "I'd be a writer. I'd write stories about people like the folks here in Whitburn. My stories would go out into the world, and somewhere two kids like you and me would read them. They'd forget for a little while that they're cold or hungry, like when we read *Little Women* by lamplight after Mam and Pap have gone to sleep."

Lem spoke quietly in my ear. "Your dream will come true one day. I know it will."

I threw my hands up in the air. "How would you know that, Lemuel David Soames?"

He shrugged. "Your name, of course. You must be named Destiny for a reason."

"Mam's fancy is the reason," I laughed.

"You *are* destined for somethin' good; I feel it. I know Mam's partial to me, and I'm sorry to you for it, but she's blind to the truth. You're the smart one; you're the one who'll get us all away from this life."

I looked into my brother's eyes and felt his words sink into my heart. I wanted to believe him, wanted to believe that he could somehow see the future. I dreamed so often of a life where we lived in a place that wasn't gray and where we weren't always hungry and cold. In my dreams, I saw Mam dressed in fine clothes and the babies with chubby faces instead of their dear little pinched ones. And Lem…

He broke the mood. Lem turned away and climbed up on the fence.

"Come on, Dess. Let's go for a ride. It'll be my last for a while."

"You know I'm scared of horses. You go on though."

Lem whistled to two horses grazing across the meadow. They immediately raised their heads and trotted over as he jumped down. He scratched each horse between the eyes and spoke softly to them. He gently slapped the smaller brown one on its rump, and it walked over to nuzzle at my pockets through the boards of the fence. Lem smiled as I backed away, and then he grabbed a handful of the mane of the larger tan horse and vaulted onto its back.

He leaned over the horse's neck and gently kicked it in the sides. They took off, cantering and then galloping across the meadow. I was scared to get on a horse, but I loved to watch Lem ride. He and the horse seemed welded into one being as they sped across the meadow and back again. Watching Lem ride across the meadow that night felt like watching a lovely poem come alive before my eyes. If I were to give a name to that poem, I would call it "Joy." I caught a glimpse of Lem's face when the moonlight hit him as he made a turn, and I had never seen him look so blissfully happy.

My heart turned over in my chest. I looked up and found my star again. "Please, oh please, let me find a way to get him out of the mine. Let me make his dream come true." I repeated my wish, my prayer, until Lem slowed the horse and trotted toward me. He jumped down and gave the horse a final pat. Then he climbed the fence, and we walked back to number five, both of us quiet and unsure about what the next days would bring, but content for the moment to be together.

Chapter Four

Mam woke Lem at four o'clock the next morning. I got up too and made him a lunch to take to the mine while Mam fixed his breakfast. She hugged him real hard as he was leaving. He looked at me over her shoulder and winked and then headed out.

This became our regular routine. I could have slept in, but getting up early and helping a bit reduced some of the guilt I felt for being able to go back to school when Lem couldn't. It didn't seem right to me that Lem had to work the mine just because he was a boy. None of this seemed right to me.

Mam put her foot down for once and told Pap that he'd have to fend for himself so I could return to school while she took the babies with her to Miz Hampton's. Mam never told me that she didn't believe Pap's story of how the fire started, but this showed me that she didn't trust Pap with C.J. and Emmie anymore.

Back at school, Miss Morrissey hugged me and told me how much she would miss Lem. I hurried to my desk that morning with a lump in my throat and spent the day trying to avoid looking at his empty desk. Miss Morrissey must have noticed because the next day, the desk was gone.

Pap took another week off to nurse his hurt arm. Sometimes when he didn't think anyone was looking, though, I'd see him using it, and I knew he was faking. The ball of black anger that had settled in my chest got stronger, especially as I saw what being in the mine was doing to my brother.

Lem never complained as the days went along, but I could tell he was miserable and exhausted. When Mam asked every evening at supper, Lem told her his day had been fine. He even told her funny stories about the other miners. Her eyes never left his face, and I could tell that even though she laughed at his stories, she was seeing the changes in him too. Lem's shoulders pulled forward now, and he was quiet unless someone asked him a question. He was turning inward on himself, and I was afraid that he was going to just shrivel up and blow away.

I rubbed his shoulders every night after we were supposed to be asleep. I pushed and pulled the knots out of his muscles so he could relax. I wanted him to tell me about the mine, but he fell asleep every night as soon as his head hit the pillow. I missed our nightly whispers.

A couple weeks after Pap had returned to work and there had been no mention of Lem quitting the mine, I woke in the middle of the night and couldn't go back to sleep. I got up, wrapped my blanket around me and went into the main room. I sat cross-legged on the floor next to the coal stove and let its warmth make me drowsy.

I became aware of words around me and realized that I could hear Mam and Pap talking quietly in their room. I knew I shouldn't eavesdrop, but Pap didn't really know how to whisper. Besides, they were talking about Lem.

"We have to get him out of the mine. Can't you see what working there is doing to him, Calton? He wasn't meant to be a miner."

"You say that like there's somethin' wrong with bein' a miner. Don't forget it's me that puts a roof over your head and food on your table."

I had to strain to hear Mam's quiet voice. "You know I'm not criticizing. Coal mining is a hard and dangerous job. Some men can handle it, and some can't. Lem isn't you, Calton. He's always been small-boned and sensitive."

"He's got to learn to handle it. Things ain't goin' to change anytime soon. The violence that ended the Harlan County strikes showed that. Men don't even whisper about formin' a union in Whitburn anymore."

"A union could make life better for you and me, but it's not the answer for Lem. Besides, you weren't always meant to be a miner either."

"Well, fate got in the way, didn't it?" Pap replied angrily.

After a pause, he said more gently, "Aw, Lil, please don't cry. There's no sense in lookin' backward now, is there? Don't you think I'd take you back to Lexington in a heartbeat if there was any chance I could work again with horses?"

"But maybe there is a chance. A lot of time has gone by. People have probably forgotten by now."

"People will never forget!" Pap said bitterly. "The name Calton Soames will always be linked with…with what happened."

"Davy Shaw would find you a spot; I know he would," said Mam.

"Davy's a good man, but even he told me to move along there at the end. I can't go back now, hat in hand, and beg for a job."

"It wouldn't be begging, and you know it. Davy was your best friend. He came through for us more than once. Besides, any stable manager would be glad to have you train for them. You were the best; even my father admitted that."

"We tried to start again years ago, and you know that didn't work out. I won't talk with you again about this, Lil." The bedsprings groaned loudly, and I imagined Pap turning his back to Mam.

I started to return to my bed when Mam's quiet voice came again. Her arguments took a new direction.

"What about our treasure, then? You could use some of it to pay off the debt to Mr. Joe, and Lem could go back to school."

Treasure? Did Pap really have a secret pot of money hidden somewhere? I perked up my ears.

"That's our rainy day fund and you know it. We vowed not to touch it unless we have to."

"Seems to me to be raining now, Calton."

"It don't hurt the boy to work. You made him too soft. I'm goin' to sleep."

I frowned in disappointment. Their secret was still hidden from me. But Mam's voice whispered again.

"Don't you think you should move it from the foot of the ash tree now that we've changed houses? I worry it's not safe there anymore."

Pap's exasperated voice reached me. "Until that house is re-built, nobody will be hangin' round that yard. I'll move it when I think it should be moved. Now go to sleep."

I waited a few more minutes to see if they would say anything else. My mind was reeling from all I had learned about my parents in that short conversation. But the late hour and the warmth of the stove made my mind fuzzy, so I stumbled back to bed.

Over the next few days, I thought about what I had overheard whenever I had a quiet moment to myself or when I was doing one of my endless, mindless chores. Although I felt there was still so much I didn't know, a few things were clear.

First, my parents had lived a life very different from the only one I knew. Before us kids were old enough to remember, they had lived in the big town of Lexington. Pap had been a horse trainer. Put Lexington and horses together, and that meant he must have trained Thoroughbred racing horses. Second, something happened that made Pap give up that life and brought us to Whitburn. I tried to guess what that something had been, but there had been no other clues. I knew it had to have been something bad if Pap's pride wouldn't let him go back there to try to work. And third, he must have put aside a good bit of money and hidden it near our old place.

You might think that knowing these things would have made me think better of my father, but they didn't. I agreed with Mam. If he had a chance at getting a better life for us, then Pap should take it. I felt he was being mule-headed. He should put us above his precious pride!

Pap should at least use some of the money to buy Lem's freedom. I thought about that over and over, and the ball of hate in my chest spread out until I could feel it all the way from the tips of my fingers down to my toes. I didn't tell Lem though. He was better off not knowing that his pa cared more for a hole filled with money than he did for his own son's future.

***

The early spring day had been especially fine. A warm sun shone brightly and matched my mood as I walked home. I was late leaving school. Miss Morrissey had asked me to stay after to talk. She had been acting funny all day, and I was afraid I had done something wrong. It turned out she had some good news. I remembered the exact words she said.

"Dessie, I have a surprise for you. Do you recall the poem I asked the class to write about Kentucky last fall?"

I nodded, trying to remember exactly which poem she was talking about.

"I hope you don't mind, but I entered your poem in a statewide contest, and guess what? You won!" She clapped her hands with delight.

"I what?" I couldn't quite take it in. I had never won anything before.

"Yes, the judges in Frankfort liked yours the best."

Oh, no. I remembered now.

"But Miss Morrissey, my poem about Kentucky wasn't...wasn't...well, it wasn't the most *complimentary* poem. Are you sure there's no mistake?"

"I'm sure. The judges felt your poem was honest and insightful. Here, see for yourself. It's in this letter." She handed me an official-looking letter with the state seal and the governor's name in the corner.

I read it three times before I fully understood. Not only had my poem been named the best in the state, but I had also won a paid trip for two to the Kentucky Derby, where the lieutenant governor would read my poem aloud before the big race.

I hugged Miss Morrissey and thanked her over and over. She told me to take the letter home to show Mam and Pap. I put it carefully in my pocket. The best part happened just as I was leaving.

"And Dessie…"

"Yes, Miss Morrissey?"

"You're a real writer now, you know."

I could feel the grin start at my mouth and move down my whole body as I practically skipped home, fingering the letter in my pocket every couple steps to make sure it was still there. I had never been so happy-proud before. I had been happy, of course. Even with a life as hardscrabble as ours, we had good times. But I had never done anything before, just by myself, to be proud of.

I burst in through the front door, eager to share my news.

"Hello, the house! I can't wait to tell you what happened to me…to…day…" I stopped short at the sight before me.

Pap and Lem stood glaring at each other while Mam twisted a handkerchief nervously in the background. They must have just arrived from the day shift, as their faces and hands were still grimy with soot. Pap's expression told me he was in a fearsome temper. Surprisingly, Lem's face said the same thing.

Pap shook a beefy finger at Lem. "I tell you, boy, I don't want McGuire comin' to me again, complainin' about your tally."

"And I told you, Pap. I'm doin' the best I can. I can't help it if I'm not a big ox like you are!"

"You can bulk yourself up. I started out a scrawny little thing, but I worked on buildin' my muscles, and now I'm one of the best miners around." Pap clapped himself on the chest with pride. He turned to Mam.

"Lil, give the boy extra servings every night at supper. He needs more meat on his bones to become like his old man."

"I won't," Lem said quietly.

"What did you say?" asked Pap menacingly.

"I said, I won't become like my old man!" Lem yelled.

Pap's face turned purple with rage. He drew back his right arm, and I watched, as though in slow motion, as his hand balled up in a fist.

"No!" I screamed and shoved Lem into the sofa.

Pap's fist connected with the side of my jaw with a sickening crunch. I tasted blood as my teeth bit the inside of my mouth.

Time sort of stopped. I felt my head snap back and then forward. I saw my books fall slowly to the floor. Even though I had known the punch was coming, part of me couldn't believe he had hit me. Pap didn't seem to be able to believe it either. He stood staring at me, his hand still in a fist and his mouth saying words that didn't come out.

Then the spell was broken. Mam and Lem yelled, and I collapsed onto the nearest chair, grabbing the side of my throbbing face. Lem put both arms around me, as though to protect me from another blow. Mam rushed to the kitchen and came back with a damp rag that she pressed to my face. They made shushing, murmuring noises at me, as though I was a baby like Emmie who needed comforting. I felt around the inside of my mouth with my tongue and was relieved to find all my teeth were whole.

None of us paid any attention to Pap until we heard the front door slam. There was no need for us to wonder where he'd gone. There was only one place in town he went to drown his sorrows. We all knew it would be hours before he came back. But as my mother cleaned up my face as best she could and my brother apologized for the thousandth time, I crumpled the letter in my pocket and started making my own plans.

Chapter Five

Two nights later, I waited until I was sure that everyone was asleep. It hadn't been hard to stay awake since my face still hurt. The swelling had gone down, but Lem told me I had a right fine bruise along my jaw line.

When I'd gone to school the day after Pap smacked me, Miss Morrissey had sucked in her breath loudly at the sight of me and gone right on teaching. The other kids accepted my story of running into a door without question. Mam and Pap never said another word at home about it. I was the only one finding it hard to forgive Pap and go on with life as usual.

Tonight, I did my best to ignore the pain and dressed quickly to the sound of my brother's steady breathing. I tiptoed from the room and listened for a few moments outside my parents' bedroom but only heard sounds of sleeping. I let myself quietly out the back door and tugged my thin jacket tighter around me.

I glanced up at the sky and noted the clouds drifting across the moon. I thought that was a good sign for the job I had to do—enough light to see by but hopefully not enough light for others to notice me. I walked quickly to the woods behind the house and started up the hill. I wanted to come to our old house from the rear, not the road.

I emerged from the woods behind number twenty and carefully scanned the yard. Nothing seemed to have changed since we had moved out. The house was dark and hollow looking. The back wall had caved in, and the roof was partially gone. I caught a faint scent of smoke on the breeze.

The ash tree lay in a patch of moonlight in the center of the yard. I circled it slowly, looking for a sign to show me where to search for the buried treasure. In a crook between two large roots lay a smooth, black stone that did not look like it had come there naturally. I gave a silent thank-you to Pap's lack of creativity as I pulled out the trowel I had borrowed from Mam's gardening tools.

I scraped dirt from the edges of the stone, and it came up easily. I dug in the dirt where the stone had been and piled the dirt as neatly as I could next to the hole. I don't know how long I dug but long enough for the moonlight to shift and for me to worry about how long I'd been away from home. Just when I thought I was going to have to give up, the trowel hit something. I pushed the trowel along the edges of what I soon realized was a metal box. I eased the box out of the hole and was glad to see there was no lock. I lifted the top off the box and moved aside the newspaper wrapping, expecting to find green bills. Instead, the moonlight shifted again and caught the shine of gold, silver and colored gems.

Hastily, I put the top back on the box and carried it to the woods. I sat down heavily on a pile of pine needles to examine the contents. The stash my parents had referred to wasn't money at all but jewelry. I had never been around jewels, of course, but for some reason I immediately knew in my bones these gems were the real thing.

For one crazy moment, I wondered if my parents had robbed a jewelry store, but then the truth dawned. I was looking at jewelry that had been given to Mam by the grandparents I had never met. A rush of anger surged through me at Pap. The rainy day fund he wouldn't touch for Lem wasn't his at all.

Carefully, I picked up each piece and lay them out on the ground. There was a pearl necklace, several smaller necklaces with gems and pearls, a bracelet with green stones, a jewel-encrusted watch, and several hatpins. And there at the bottom of the box lay a brooch that took my breath away. It was fashioned in the shape of a galloping golden horse.

Arcing above the horse were five jewels set into golden stars. Each star contained a jewel of a different color, with the jewel directly over the horse's head being a brilliant, clear gem that I supposed was a diamond.

I wasted several precious moments staring at the brooch. I had never seen anything so lovely before. I conjured up an image of Mam in a flowing dress with this pin on her shoulder. She must have been stunning when she was younger, before Pap and us children and hard times came along.

Mam! With these jewels, she could leave Pap. She could take Lem, C.J., Emmie and me away from this life with an angry man who drank too much. Why didn't she do that? What made her prefer life with Pap to life with parents who could buy her things like this? And not only her; our grandparents would be able to provide for my siblings and me too. I didn't understand it. I didn't understand *her*. I would have sworn that Mam would have done anything for her children, but apparently she put Pap above the four of us. I felt a sudden pain in my chest, and tears pricked my eyes.

I dashed them away angrily. In a way, finding this out about Mam made my task easier. I was going to have to harden my heart toward Mam and the little ones for a while if my plan was going to work.

I became aware of the cold seeping into my legs, which reminded me that the night was running out and I still had much to do. I put each piece of jewelry back into the newspaper bundle except for the horse brooch. Although I would hate to consider it, the individual stones could be cut off and sold if needed. I hoped it wouldn't come to that, but the whole point of digging up the stash had been to get money to put back as a safety net. Since I hadn't found any money, I had to take the next best thing.

I put the lid back on the box and carried it carefully to its hiding place. I shoveled the dirt back in the hole and pushed the black stone into place. I brushed away loose dirt and did my best to make it look like it hadn't been disturbed. At last, I sat back on my heels, reached for the brooch and pinned it to the inside of my jacket. I stood up, brushed the dirt from my hands and headed home.

I didn't go into the house right away. Instead, I went into the outhouse and pulled out Pap's shaving mirror and Mam's scissors from my dress pocket. I hung the mirror up on a nail that was there for clothes and slanted it down so I could look at my own face. I picked up one of my long brown braids, took a deep breath and snipped off the braid right below my ear. Soft brown curls suddenly sprang up around half my head.

I repeated the process on the other side and then twisted and turned to see as much of my head as I could. I had meant to cut my hair so I'd look like a boy, but it was so curly that the effect seemed even more girlish than my long braids. I thought I should cut more hair off, but I just couldn't bring myself to do it. I decided I'd stuff my hair up in one of Lem's caps instead.

I tossed the braids down the outhouse hole and slipped back into the house to return the mirror and scissors. I left the note I had written for Mam in her coffee cup, where I knew she would see it. I debated for a moment and then stood on tiptoe to reach behind the bread tin where Pap hid his hunting knife. I brought it carefully down and unsheathed it. The knife was a fearsome-looking thing with a blade that Pap sharpened every Saturday. I had never been allowed to touch it, let alone hold it. I couldn't quite believe my own actions as I sheathed the blade and strapped the knife to the outside of my right thigh with a strip of cloth from Mam's ragbag. I didn't want to think I might have need of the knife, but I felt braver as I stood up, feeling its heavy weight against my leg.

The next step in my plan would be the trickiest. I had to get Lem away without anyone hearing in that crackerjack box of a house. I took off my shoes and tiptoed into our bedroom. I grabbed Lem's tweed cap and stuffed my hair up in it, then gently shook Lem awake.

"What's…what's wrong?"

"Nothin's wrong, Lem," I whispered. "Do me a favor though. Get dressed and meet me out back, okay?"

He sighed in exasperation, but I knew he'd do it. Sometimes I would drag him from bed to watch the stars and moon, but that was usually in the summer when it's too hot to sleep. No matter; Lem had been following my lead for as long as either of us could remember.

I waited behind the house, and sure enough, Lem joined me in a couple minutes, tugging on a jacket and cap.

"Okay, Dess. What are you up to?"

I turned toward the woods, and he followed. I picked up a rag-tied bundle and handed it to him.

"Here, you carry this one. We're goin' on an adventure." I picked up a second bundle and started down the hill through the woods.

"What kind of adventure?" he whispered loudly, not moving.

"I can't tell you yet," I tossed over my shoulder and kept going.

Behind me, I heard Lem give another exasperated sigh, but he jogged down the hill until he caught up with me.

"When can you tell me?"

"When we're more than halfway there, so you won't go back."

"I don't suppose you'll tell me where 'there' is either?"

"I don't suppose so." I grinned at him, and he rolled his eyes.

***

Lem balked on me when we reached the train rails.

"Dess, I need to sleep if I'm gettin' up at four to work my shift. What's this all about?"

Instead of answering, I asked him a question. "Do you trust me?"

"That's not an answer."

"Yes, it is. Now do you trust me or not?"

His blue eyes met my brown ones. "You know I do."

"Well then. You ain't gettin' up at four to do a shift in the mine ever again. You and me are done with Whitburn and Pap and Joe Hampton."

Lem got all fidgety when he heard that. "Dess, if you mean for us to run away, we can't do that!"

I stuck my busted chin in the air. "We already are doin' it. You said I was smart, and I've got it all figured out."

"Look, I understand about you wantin' to get away from Pap after he hit you, but I think he's truly sorry."

"He ain't said so, and besides, this is about you, not me," I said. "Lem, that mine is killin' you, and I can't stand by and watch it happen."

"What about Mam and the little ones? We can't just leave them."

I felt tears prick at the back of my eyes again, but I pushed away thoughts of the babies. I was doing this for them too. "We'll send for them once we've got a new place."

"How will we get a new place? We ain't got money."

"I've got my rag and bottle money that I've saved up. Nine dollars and forty-one cents; practically a fortune. Besides, that'll get us to where we need to go." I started walking down the middle of the train track. The rail line that ran to and from the Clover Creek Mine was the shortest route to the next county.

"Dess! Just where is it you think we need to go?" Lem called after me.

"Walk with me and I'll tell you," I yelled back.

***

"So here's the low-down," I told my brother once he caught up with me. "Your dream will come true. We're headin' to Lexington."

Lem smacked his forehead with the palm of his hand. "Are you crazy?" He looked at my determined expression. "Yes, you are crazy! We're just kids. No big-time stable is goin' to hire me, and besides, it takes trainin'

65

to become a jockey. And if you haven't noticed, there's a Depression on, which means that grown people can't find work. We'll just wander around until your money runs out. Not to mention that Lexington is at least a hundred and fifty miles from here."

He paced back and forth several times while I waited for him to calm down.

"I told you, I've got it planned out. You're almost sixteen and can pass for eighteen if you need to. Plus, we won't wander around." I played my trump card. "We have a contact!" I said triumphantly.

"Who? We don't know anybody who works with horses."

"We don't, Lem, but Pap and Mam do." I hurried to tell him about the conversation I had overheard. I left out the part about the jewelry. I didn't feel guilty for borrowing the brooch, but I felt sure Lem wouldn't like me taking it. "So, we'll go meet this Davy Shaw and tell him who we are, and he'll watch you ride, and then he's sure to give you a job." Without thinking, I took off the cap I was wearing and slapped it against my thigh.

"That is such a long shot and…and…and just what did you do to your hair?!"

I spent the next few minutes explaining why I had cut my hair, and by the time that conversation was over, we had passed through the tiny town of Gretchen. We were more than halfway to Hayward. And in Hayward, there was a passenger train station. I smiled grimly to myself. There was no going back for Lem and me now, at least not without a whipping for both of us. I tucked my arm through Lem's and picked up our pace. He matched me step for step, as he'd always done.

Chapter Six

The sun was rising as we entered the outskirts of Hayward. The few times I'd been allowed to come with Mam and Pap, we'd mostly visited the town square, so I knew how to find the train station. Hayward was the county seat. Shops and restaurants surrounded the courthouse, although I noticed more boarded-up windows than I'd seen the last time I'd been there. The train station was located a block over from the courthouse. I didn't know what time trains started going in and out of stations, but I wanted to be sure we wouldn't miss the one to Lexington. We were both yawning when we hauled ourselves up to the station. The sign on the door said the station opened at 8:00 a.m.

We argued a bit about what time we thought it was and then decided to go around the back and wait where other people would be less likely to see us. I didn't want to bring too much attention to what we were doing, but I had a story ready in case any adult wondered where our parents might be.

Lem found a spot at the side of the station behind some crates where we could sit and rest until the stationmaster showed up. I unpacked two biscuits and chunks of cheese from my bundle, and we ate that for breakfast, choking the food down dry. But sitting there with Lem watching the sun rise, I thought our meager breakfast was quite wonderful, even if I was feeling as tired as I'd ever been in my life.

"Dess, you look worn to pieces. Lay against my shoulder and take a nap."

"I don't think I should. As soon as the station opens, we'll need to find out the train schedule."

"I'll keep watch. You get some sleep."

"But you need sleep too."

"You're the one who was up half the night gettin' ready for this adventure. I got more sleep than you. I'll stay awake, and next time it'll be your turn to keep watch."

I looked at Lem doubtfully, but he was right. My nighttime exertions were catching up with me. I couldn't stifle the yawn as I nodded and snuggled up against him.

"Be sure to wake me up at the first … sign … of… peo…ple…" I mumbled before sleep carried me away.

***

Slowly, I became aware of noises around me. The noises were strange—not the noises I usually heard when I awoke. I could hear lots of people talking in different conversations, and somewhere someone was calling out places and times. A whistle blew shrilly, and I sat up quickly, jostling my brother, who was asleep next to me.

I punched him on the arm. "Lem! You fell asleep. Oh my mercy, we may have missed our train!"

Lem opened his eyes and was immediately remorseful. "I'm so sorry. I didn't mean to fall asleep. Let's go see what time it is."

"Yes, but we need to leave here carefully, one at a time. I'll go first and meet you out on the platform in a minute."

I peeked over the crates in front of us. No one seemed to be around, so I got up and inched my way to the corner. Travelers stood in small groups or lounged on benches, their luggage at their feet. A line had formed at the ticket window at the other end of the platform. As I watched, a man in a uniform came out of the station and bellowed, "Four-thirty to Nashville." People started bustling around, picking up their belongings and shuffling toward the edge of the platform.

A bench near me emptied, so I hurried there and sat down, spreading out to keep others off. As the train thundered into view and came to a stop, Lem joined me on the bench.

"Four-thirty," I hissed at him. "Hells bells, Lem. We slept the whole darn day away!"

His eyes widened in shock. "Destiny Rose Soames! Don't go cussin' at me. I said I was sorry and meant it, but what would Mam do if she heard you?"

I rolled my eyes. We had bigger worries than me cussing. "I don't give a fig. Now stay here while I go check the schedule and see if we can still catch a train to Lexington today." I left my bundle next to Lem, started toward the ticket window and then turned back. "And if any adult asks you where our parents are, tell them our grandma dropped us off to get on a train home. Think you can do that right?"

He nodded with a hurt look in his eyes, but I ignored it. I was worried, so I let my worry look like I was steamed. I wasn't just afraid we'd missed our chance to catch a train, but I was also worried that the time we had wasted would give Mam and Pap time to come find us—if they tried to, that is. I wondered about that. I felt that Mam would want to chase us and bring us home, but I wasn't sure about Pap. Maybe he'd just as soon not have us to feed anymore. Maybe us leaving would be a good thing in his eyes. I shrugged. I just didn't know what to think, so it was better to leave those thoughts alone.

I smoothed down my skirt and tried to look like I belonged alone on a train platform as I weaved my way around the groups of travelers. I found a spot near the line at the ticket window where I could clearly read the schedule over the head of the man selling tickets. I sagged in relief when I saw there was a train to Lexington due in soon and hurried back to Lem.

I drew up short when I saw that he had let someone sit next to him in my place. A young man with black hair who looked to be a couple years older than my brother was speaking animatedly with Lem. As I walked near, he glanced up and grinned at me, green eyes crinkling in the corners.

He stuck out his hand. "This must be your sister. You didn't tell me she was so pretty, Lem." At his words, my heart seemed to constrict in my chest. "Hi there, Dessie. My name's Brendan Cole. Glad to meet you."

The smile he beamed my way was dazzling. In a bit of a daze, I shook his hand and wondered if I imagined it when he lingered a bit longer than he should before letting it go.

Confused, I turned to Lem. "Have you met before?"

"Oh, no, we just met. Brendan's from Gretchen and on his way back to Chattanooga. He's in college there."

I looked at Brendan's dungarees and frayed cuffs. He didn't look like what I imagined a college boy to be.

He must have noticed my expression because he hurried to say, "These are my at-ease clothes, don't you know. When you've ridden as many trains as I have, you learn it's best to be as comfortable as you can on the rails. I was just telling your brother that I'm an old hand at train travel, and I'll be glad to give you two some tips, since your grandma couldn't stay to see you off and all."

I glanced at Lem and he nodded, proud of himself for keeping to our cover story. Brendan scooted over and waved me to the spot between himself and Lem. He sure was the handsomest boy I'd ever seen. Much more handsome even than Bobby Wilcox back in Whitburn, who all the girls swooned over. I sat down, but I was still wary.

"What kind of tips can you give us?"

"Well," he winked at me, "when you go buy your tickets, bend your knees so you look shorter, and ask for two children's tickets at half-fare. Then when the conductor comes around when you're on the train, tuck your legs up under you, and if he asks, say your mother just left for the dining car."

"Say, that's pretty clever."

My brother shook his head. "Sounds kind of dishonest to me."

"Lem, we need to be careful with our money. If we can buy half-price tickets, it would stretch further. What Brendan is suggestin' is like gettin' a sale on the tickets."

Brendan coughed and took out a monogrammed handkerchief that he dabbed daintily at his mouth. "Speaking of being careful with your money…"

"Yeah?"

"Well, I don't mean to pry, of course, but you should know that crooks try to steal money in train stations. Uhm, how are you carrying your money?"

"Oh," I said, dismissively, "it's safe. I've got it wrapped in a handkerchief in my pocket."

Brendan laughed and then apologized. "I am sorry. I don't mean to criticize, but only real country bumpkins carry their money that way. A pickpocket could clean you out in no time flat!"

"How should we carry our money?" Lem asked, and I nodded.

Brendan opened his jacket and showed us a leather pouch strapped to his belt. "See this? No pickpocket is going to get at my money without me knowing about it. This is the safe way to carry money around. Believe me, I learned the hard way."

"So you were robbed on a train?" asked Lem, his eyes widening.

Our new friend nodded. "Yep, on my way home last time. Fellow bumped into me as I was boarding. I didn't realize what had happened until I went to the dining car. He cleaned me out. I had to wash a few dishes to pay for my dinner that day."

Lem nudged me. "Sure wish we had one of those pouches, don't you, Dess?"

I guess I was busy staring at Brendan because Lem had to nudge me a second time before I said, "Sure, sure do."

Brendan looked around the platform as though he was afraid other people might hear, and then he leaned in close, lowering his voice. I was so distracted by his nearness that I was a bit slow to understand his words.

"Well, listen. I just happen to have an extra pouch on me. I was going to give it to my roommate back at college, but heck, you two are so nice, and I'd like to help you out. I'll sell it to you for a dollar." He held out a thin brown pouch.

I came to full attention when he said the word *dollar*. Lem was already reaching for the pouch. "Now hold up there, Lem. That's a lot of money to spend. I don't know if we should."

"But if we don't buy it, we could lose all our money. You heard what happened to Brendan."

I looked from my brother's trusting face to the face of this handsome stranger. He seemed to be honest and open. I guessed we could take the chance.

"Well, all right. We'll take it." Brendan nodded as I dug deep in my dress pocket and pulled out the handkerchief-wrapped bundle. I unwrapped it and handed a dollar to Brendan.

"Thanks," he said and winked at me again as he pocketed the money. "Here, let me show you how to use this."

Brendan took the bills out of my hand and stuffed them in the pouch. He zipped it up tightly.

A man on the platform nearby started yelling at one of the railroad workers. He seemed to be upset about a train that was running late. People moved away from him when he waved his arms about wildly, but the stationmaster came over to talk to him, and he settled down. They walked into the station together.

Lem and I turned back to Brendan. "Some people have no class," he said. "Now, Lem needs to be the one to carry the money pouch. Just strap it on your belt right there."

"Look, Dessie," Lem patted the slightly bulging pouch on his belt. "Ain't that sweet?"

"It'll do. Thank you, Brendan."

He made an exaggerated bow. "At your service, my lady." I giggled. "Well, I need to be moving on. My train is due in an hour, and I want to get supper across the street first. Care to join me?"

"Our train will be here in a couple minutes," I said hastily, "but thanks again."

He grinned at us, nodded a farewell and sauntered away. I watched him until he turned the corner toward the front of the station and then realized we hadn't bought our tickets.

I tugged at Lem's jacket, and he followed me to the ticket line. When we reached the window, I asked for two tickets at the children's fare price, as Brendan had suggested. Lem frowned but unzipped the pouch and pulled out two bills, handed them to the man and waited for his change.

"Say, what game you playin', sonny?" demanded the man. "This ain't money. You just handed me two pieces of paper."

"What?" we both cried at once.

Lem dug into the money pouch. He pulled out a wad of green, but as he thumbed through it, we both saw that it was plain paper, not money.

"I don't understand," said my brother.

"I do. That Brendan Cole, if that is his name, is a no-good swindler! He stole our money, Lem."

"Brendan? No, maybe there's some mistake."

"The only mistake was yours in talkin' to that crook in the first place! How many times do I have to tell you that you can't trust strangers?" My voice rose to a screech, and I was close to what Pap liked to call hysterics.

"You two get along there," said the ticket man. "Other folks with money need to buy tickets."

Lem grabbed my hand and pulled me to an empty bench near the edge of the platform. I flopped down in a temper.

"I can't believe it; I just can't believe it!"

"You saved bottles and rags and sold them for two years to get that money, Dessie, and I go and lose it all at once. How could I be so stupid?" Lem hung his head dejectedly.

"I was taken in by him, too, you know." I punched Lem on the arm.

"We better just head home now. I appreciate what you tried to do, but I think this adventure is over."

"Give me a minute to think."

As we sat there in misery, the train to Lexington rolled in. We watched in wretched silence as travelers around us picked up their luggage and boarded the train. I looked away and gazed down the line of cars. I noticed a man in ragged clothes step up to an open boxcar and climb in. I could tell by the furtive way he was looking around that he was sneaking on as a stowaway.

The train whistle blew, and the train belched black smoke and started to pull out of the station. At the same moment, I spied Pap. He was inside the building talking to the stationmaster. I knew he'd come for us, and in that instant, I also knew going back with him was the last thing I wanted to do.

I grabbed Lem's arm and hauled him to his feet. I pushed him to the edge of the platform and grabbed his hand.

"Lem, we're still gettin' on this train. Jump when I say to."

"No, we can't…"

Pap was coming out the door. The open boxcar pulled alongside the platform. It was now or never.

"Jump!" I yelled and tugged Lem with me. We jumped together.

"Dessie!" Pap's cry faded quickly behind us.

Chapter Seven

We were tangled in a heap of arms, legs and bundles. Laughing at the relief of being alive and unhurt, we hugged and babbled directions to each other to get untangled until we slowly became aware of faces around us, silent and staring.

The boxcar was dim and shadowy, but I could make out about a dozen men sitting or lounging around the walls. Their faces were grim and their bodies were tense, and I could feel the hair on the back of my neck rise.

Lem didn't notice the tension in the boxcar. "Hello there," he called out. "Nice to meet you gentlemen. My name's Lem, and this is my sister Dessie. Boy, that was some jump, don't you think?"

No one answered; they just kept staring. Lem got to his feet uncertainly and then helped me up. I was seriously regretting my impulsive move.

Suddenly, I felt strong arms go around me, pinning my arms to my sides. I screamed in fear and surprise.

Lem yelled, "Hey there!" and made a grab at the man holding me. The man pushed him away so strongly that Lem was thrown back and hit the floor of the boxcar with a loud thud.

"Lem!" I yelled and tried to wrench myself free to go to him. The arms held me fast.

"You're a pretty little thing, ain't you?" the man growled into my ear. He twisted me around to face him, and I caught the distinct smell of moonshine on his breath. I was looking into a grubby face grizzled with stubble. "Now stop your squirmin'. I just want a little kiss is all, right boys?" He called this last over his shoulder. Chuckling and whistles broke out from some of the other men.

A couple of the men moved in closer to us. "Please help me," I begged, but the ones near just nudged one another and laughed.

I shrank down in horror as a mouth with teeth stained with tobacco juice came near, and I fumbled for the knife on my thigh. I raised the hem of my dress and grabbed the hilt of the knife with my right hand as I raised my left hand and shoved it in the man's face. I hesitated to pull out the knife though. Part of me just wasn't sure if I could actually stick it in another person's body.

"Stop this!" said a deep voice. The arms around me hesitated and then let up, and I felt a rush of relief as I pushed the knife back in its sheath. I twisted away from my captor and rushed to Lem's side. He was struggling to get up.

"I think my ankle's twisted, Dess," he whispered. "I landed on it funny."

"Shh, it'll be all right," I said automatically, my attention on the two men staring each other down in the center of the boxcar. The ring around them widened as the other men returned to their seats.

My savior was a tall, copper-haired man with wide shoulders and muscles that bulged within his rough work shirt. As we watched, he clapped a huge hand on the shoulder of the man who had pushed Lem.

"Shorty, I know you didn't mean any harm, but you scared the boy and the little girl. Now say you're sorry, and we can welcome them proper. This ain't the way to show the hospitality of the rails."

The one called Shorty took a gulp and doffed his cap, saying, "Sure, sure, Red. I didn't mean no harm." He turned toward us. "Beggin' your pardon, miss, I'm sure." He smiled at me, showing his brown teeth, but the smile didn't reach his eyes, and I shivered at the sight of it.

"Now that's better. We may be down on our luck, but we can still show folks good manners. I reckon you'll give Lem and Dessie their privacy, won't you?" Red's words were polite, but I could tell he wasn't really asking a question. Shorty nodded. "And that goes for the rest of you lot, too, or you'll have me to answer to." The big man jerked a thumb at his massive chest.

I flopped down next to Lem and gently probed his ankle. He winced but didn't cry out. "I'll wrap it up tight soon as I can, but you'll have to rest it, I reckon," I whispered.

"Are you hurt, son?" the deep voice asked. I looked up to see the man called Red towering over us.

Lem reached up a hand. "Thank you, sir, for helpin' us. I hurt my ankle when I fell, but I'll be fine soon."

The man solemnly shook Lem's hand and reached down to lift my brother. "Let's move you two over here to the corner. I've got a nice spot I can share."

I started to protest, but he waved my words away and half-carried Lem to the empty back wall next to a corner. He gently put him down with his hurt ankle stretched out. I noticed the spot he took us to had blankets and other gear lying about, and none of the other men had taken spots nearby.

I knelt next to Lem and put one of the rag bundles under his foot to elevate the ankle.

The big man folded himself into a sitting position in front of us and screened us from the sight of the other men. "My name's Albert Timmons, but as you heard, everyone calls me Red. And you are Lem and Dessie, if I heard correct."

I nodded. "Pleased to meet you, Mr. Red, and thank you for coming to my rescue from that nasty man." I shuddered at the memory of his tight arms and dirty mouth.

"Glad to be of service, miss. Now what brings you two into my humble abode?" He opened his arms and offered us a mock bow. Lem smiled, but from the sweat on his brow, I knew his ankle was hurting bad.

"We're goin' to Lexington to get work on a horse farm."

"We?" Lem asked me. "I thought I was the one lookin' for a job."

"Well, since most of our money just got stolen, we both need to work, don't we?" I asked a bit too sarcastically.

Lem hung his head. "I should have known Brendan was a crook."

"He was a no-good, stinkin', yellow-bellied rat-fink is what he was!"

Mr. Red chimed in. "Hold on here. Were you robbed?"

"Just now. I was waitin' for Dess to check the train schedule when this fellow came over. He said he lived nearby, and he seemed real nice. He said he'd help us keep our money safe and offered to sell us this money pouch, but when we went to buy our tickets, all that was in it was green paper, see?" Lem held out the pouch for Mr. Red to examine.

"Yep, he pulled a switcheroo on you. He would have had two pouches, you see, and when you weren't lookin', he switched yours for this one and walked away with your money. Rat-fink is right, Dessie." Mr. Red nodded to me.

"I can't figure out when he did the switch though," said Lem.

"I can. Lem, you remember, right when Brendan was holdin' our money pouch, that man started yellin' on the platform? We both watched him for a few seconds at least. I bet he was the rat-fink's partner!"

"That's probably right. Most of these small-time crooks work in pairs. So...you couldn't buy tickets and decided to catch a ride instead?"

"Dessie had us jump. For a second there, I thought we were goners!" Lem laughed.

Mr. Red looked at us sternly. "You do know how dangerous that was, right? If your ma or pa knew, they'd skin your hides. We just met, but I want you to promise me you won't do that again."

I felt the color rise up my neck like it always does when I feel guilty about something. I could have gotten us both killed with that stunt. And then I had landed us in more of a soup with the dust-up with the man called Shorty. If it hadn't been for Mr. Red, no telling what would have happened to us. I didn't really want to suppose either.

I raised my chin up. "It was my fault. I'm always gettin' Lem into scrapes. But that was a full-on daft thing to do, and I'll be more careful from now on. I promise."

Mr. Red nodded and smiled, and I thought maybe he might do me one more favor.

"Mr…Red, sir, I'd like to…to change clothes. If you could hold up that blanket there, I could change in this corner."

Mr. Red jumped right up and held up the blanket he'd been sitting on. I ducked behind it and took out Lem's clothes that I had brought for myself. When I pulled on the pair of flannels, I realized I wouldn't be able to grab the knife. I considered changing its location but then decided to tear out the bottom of the right pocket instead. I put the pants back on and reached for the knife through the pocket. That worked right well, and I felt a small comfort in knowing I could get to it easily if I needed to. I pulled on a sweater and my jacket, tucked my hair up under the cap and came back out from behind the blanket.

Lem wasn't impressed with my new look. "First you've made us into hobos, and now you turn yourself into a fellow? Dess, maybe we need to give up on this adventure."

I sat down next to my brother and tore my slip into strips. I wound the strips around Lem's sprained ankle. "We've come this far. I think we should at least try to get work in Lexington. And see, if folks think I'm a boy, I'm more likely to get hired," I pleaded.

"If you two are goin' to ride the rails like us other wanderers—the gents and me don't really like the term hobo, son—it ain't a bad idea for Dessie to dress like a boy. Bad sorts like Shorty there won't be tryin' to steal kisses, for one thing. Now, let's get some supper together and talk over this plan of yours."

Mr. Red opened a can of cold beans, and I unbundled bread and fruit. After all he'd done for us, sharing our food was the least we could do. While we ate, Mr. Red told us about his life as a wanderer. He had roamed from town to town looking for work for three years, ever since his wife died from influenza and the bank foreclosed on his farm. He had spent nights in jail for jumping trains until he learned which rail lines had guards check for extra riders and which ones didn't. He had won many brawls in boxcars with other riders, but most knew him by reputation now, so he was left alone. Mr. Red liked to work with animals, too, since he'd been a farmer, and he'd worked a stint at a stable in Lexington the year before. I told him about Lem being so good with horses and asked if he knew Davy Shaw.

"No, can't say I've heard the name. But if you're set on this plan, you should go to the Bluegrass Breeders' Syndicate office once we get to town. It's only a couple blocks from the station. They can tell you what horse farm Davy Shaw works for."

He glanced at Lem, who was dozing now. "But Dessie, take my advice. If he won't help you, turn around and go home. These are dark times. Work's hard to come by, and that makes men desperate. As bad as you might think your home is, it's got to be better than ridin' these rails."

I nodded. "And I doubt you're handy enough with that knife for it to offer much protection," he whispered.

I glanced at him in surprise.

"I saw you reach for it when Shorty grabbed you," he said softly. "I've learned some things the hard way, and one of them is that you don't pull a knife on somebody unless you're prepared to use it." He motioned for me to lean back. "You get some sleep now. None of the fellows will bother us, and you'll need your rest for tomorrow."

"All right, Mr. Red. Goodnight."

"Goodnight, little miss." Our protector lay on the dirty floor in front of Lem and me, hemming us in a safe wedge in the corner of the boxcar. He turned his back to us and was soon snoring peacefully.

I leaned back against the wall of the boxcar and put one arm around Lem's shoulders. He stirred and asked, sleepily, "That was Pap, wasn't it, at the station? I heard his voice."

"Yes," I whispered. "Are you mad at me for making you jump?"

He shook his head. "No. I've been thinkin'. I told you back at the Hamptons' field that I think your name means there's a purpose for you that's bigger than life in Whitburn. Maybe this is it. Maybe we are supposed to go on this adventure to find your destiny, yours and mine. So I'm all in, Dess."

That was Lem. Just when I thought he'd given up, he'd come shining through with such trust in me. I gave him a quick hug. "I hope you're right."

"But I wonder about Pap. Was he there because he was mad or because he missed us?"

"Missed your wages from the mine, more likely. Hush now and go back to sleep."

Lem slid down to the floor, and I lay down behind him, his back to my front. His breathing was soon even, and I knew he was asleep again, but I lay looking at the night sky through a small vent in the top of the wall of the boxcar above me. A bright star shone down through the opening. I knew it was my star, my wishing star, and I smiled to greet it.

I thought about all that had happened today. It seemed like a lifetime ago that we had left the house instead of a few short hours. I had been so sure when we set out. I thought I had it planned so carefully, but a charming smile and a pair of green eyes had distracted me, and we'd lost the money I'd saved. If Pap hadn't shown up just when he did, I'd probably have taken Lem back home.

I stared at my star without seeing it. *If Pap hadn't shown up just when he did*...we wouldn't have jumped into this boxcar at just the right time. *Destiny*. Lem had used that word, my name. I'd never really thought about the meaning of my name before other than to be embarrassed by it and to insist, loudly and repeatedly, to be called Dessie. Now I considered it. A destiny was a future that was bound to happen, no matter what. Maybe my destiny was to get Lem out of Whitburn. And maybe this plan, that looked like it was going wrong, was actually going right. Maybe we were supposed to meet up with Brendan and Mr. Red for reasons I just couldn't see yet. And if that were true, then we were going to be all right. We were going to find Davy Shaw and a better life in Lexington.

I sent a wish to my star to be on the safe side. I patted the knife at my thigh too. A destiny is all well and good, but a sharp blade gives a girl wanderer extra peace of mind.

Chapter Eight

Something sharp was poking me in the neck when I awoke early the next morning. I unwrapped my arms from around Lem and sat up. My arms and legs felt stiff, and I winced at the movement as I tucked the hair that had come loose in the night under my cap. I pulled my jacket away and saw the star horse brooch pinned to the inside. I'd forgotten all about it. I closed my jacket quickly so no one else could see the jewels.

I looked around and found Mr. Red sitting against the side of the boxcar, smiling at me. He handed me a steaming cup, and I gratefully took a sip of the coffee and felt its warmth course through my body. I gazed at his kind face and knew he wasn't interested in robbing me of the pin, even if he had seen it. When I finished the coffee, Mr. Red poured another cup for Lem and then busied himself with dousing his small fire.

I shook Lem's shoulder. "Lem, get up. We get off the train soon."

Lem shifted around and opened his piercing blue eyes. "Mornin', Dessie." He scooted into a sitting position, and I handed him the coffee.

"Oh, that tastes good. Is there any more bread?"

I dug in my bundle and came up with a chunk that I divided into three pieces. "Yes, here's breakfast." I handed a piece to our new friend.

"Thankee kindly," he said and turned to Lem. "How's that ankle?"

Lem stretched out his leg and grimaced. "It's still sore, but I think I can walk on it."

"Well, just to be on the safe side, I'll help you off the train. We'll be in Lexington in about a half an hour. We'll need to get off before we reach the station but not too soon or the jump is too hard. There's an art, you see, to timin' the departure just right." Mr. Red winked.

"Is that something you learned the hard way?" I asked.

"Yup. Now finish up your breakfast and get your bits and pieces packed away."

We watched as Mr. Red carefully but quickly packed his gear. His blanket had pockets in it where he stowed his coffeepot and flint, bowl, cup, food and canteen. He rolled up his extra set of clothes and put them on top. Mr. Red then folded it all into a pack that he strapped onto his back with two belts, with his belongings neatly stored inside, close to his body. Lastly, he picked up a stout walking stick leaning against the wall of the boxcar.

"That's a neat trick, Mr. Red," said Lem. "Sure wish we had met up with you before our money got stolen, don't you, Dessie?"

"Yeah, but we'll be all right. My wishing star told me so last night."

Mr. Red gave me a funny look, but Lem just nodded and started packing up our few belongings. We each tied up a bundle, put it over a forearm and went to stand at the open door to the boxcar when Mr. Red called us over.

The dawn was breaking as the train began to slow. We were in the city now, and I watched as the buildings we passed became taller and closer together. Despite our situation, I felt a thrill of excitement at the sight of the stores and warehouses, cars and trucks, sidewalks and streets. I'd never been in a city before. I remembered Mr. Red's warning from the night before, but it only added an edge to my eagerness to explore this new world.

Mr. Red's voice spoke in my ear. "This door faces away from the station. I'll help Lem down first. When he's on the ground, I'll turn back for you, but you'll have to jump. Okay?"

I looked down at the tracks still whizzing by at a steady clip and felt my breakfast become stone in my stomach. But I nodded, since it was the only way off the train, and stuffed my hands in my pockets to stop their sudden shaking.

Mr. Red sat down on the edge of the boxcar and dangled his legs over. Lem sat down next to him and gave me a thumbs-up sign over Mr. Red's shoulder. Behind us, I could hear the others talking and preparing to leave too.

Without warning, Mr. Red jumped. He and Lem tumbled together, with Mr. Red's big hands protecting Lem's blond head. Mr. Red sat up and called, "Now, Dessie!"

Again I looked down at the tracks, and the ground became a blur before my eyes. I couldn't do it. I was sure I'd miss somehow and end up under the huge iron wheels of the train. Just then I felt a hot palm on my shoulder. I looked around quickly and found Shorty grinning at me. I shoved him away and jumped out of the train in the same quick movement. I hit the ground and bent my knees, grabbing them with my hands to create a ball of my body. I rolled a few times and came to a stop. I surveyed myself before I opened my eyes. I was alive and okay.

Mr. Red rushed up while Lem hobbled a bit behind.

"Dessie, for a second there, we weren't sure you would jump!" Lem said as he gave me a hug.

"I wasn't so sure either until I realized I couldn't stay in the train with Shorty on it." I laughed and shuddered at the same time.

"All right, my dears, let's go over yonder, away from the tracks. Patrols may come around." Mr. Red pointed, and we followed him into a nearby alley as the other men who'd been in our boxcar leaped out farther along the tracks and darted off in different directions.

"This is where we part company, I'm afraid," said our friend with a sad smile. "I'm bound for St. Louis. Dessie, the place you want is that way." He gestured with his stick.

I nodded. My throat was thick with unshed tears as I watched Lem hold out his hand. Now it was my turn to say goodbye. I threw my arms around Mr. Red.

"Oh, how can we ever thank you? You saved us! Why were you so kind?"

Mr. Red patted my back. "In another life, I had a little girl of my own. She was just about your age when she…when we parted. If she was ever among strangers and needed help, I would hope someone would be there. It was my pleasure, Dessie. You and Lem take care of yourselves, you hear?"

"We hear," we said together and laughed. "Goodbye, Mr. Red."

My brother and I turned away and walked in the direction our friend had shown us. Lem limped a bit, so our progress was slow. When we reached the next corner, I looked back, but Mr. Red had vanished. We were on our own again.

We turned the corner and started looking for the Bluegrass Breeders' offices. I figured it would be in one of the tall brick buildings we were passing, but we couldn't find a sign for it. In the third block down, we came upon a long line of men waiting to go into a one-story, dingy-looking building. We walked up to the last man in the line.

"Hey, mister, what's this line for?" I asked in my deepest voice.

The man looked surprised. "Where have you been, son? This is the line for horse farm jobs. Every Friday, the managers come in and pick new workers."

"Thankee," I said and touched my cap to him.

"This is what we were lookin' for," I said to my brother.

"What do we do now, Dess?"

"I reckon we wait, Lem. And from now on, you better call me Denny."

We waited for at least a couple hours in the slow-moving line. More raggedy men and boys came and stood behind us until the line stretched a good city block. I was nervous about whether I could pull off being a boy, so I kept quiet and listened to the conversations going on around us. The men passed rumors of possible jobs in other places. They shared tips on where a free bed could be found for the night and what the menu was that day at the nearest soup kitchen.

I looked at the ragged hats and coats, the shoes with newspapers sticking out of the soles, the patched shirts and pants around me. I saw the lines of anxiety and hunger in the faces. I realized that like the men in the boxcar, these were all desperate men. For the first time, I felt the impact of the Depression. It had just been a word to me before. But here were people who were suffering. Maybe they had been respectable, hardworking folk once. Now, through no fault of their own, they didn't even know where their next meal was coming from.

Maybe they had families to feed, like Pap did. The thought came to me that perhaps Pap had been so hard toward us because his life was hard. He had the responsibility of taking care of five other people. I looked at Lem and knew he was depending on me, like we had depended on Pap. I sent a prayer up that Davy Shaw would be glad to meet us and help us, and I rubbed my finger over the spot on my jacket where the brooch was hidden. It was my safety net, my way to take care of Lem if my other plans didn't work out.

When the line had shortened to just a handful of men, a man in a striped suit came out and yelled that the breeders were done hiring for the day. The disappointment around us was keen, with some men cursing loudly and others just walking away, silent and grim.

I hurried to the man in the suit and tugged on his arm. "Excuse me, sir, but we have different business. Is there someone we can talk to?"

The man looked down at me and sneered around a cigar in his mouth, "What kind of business, sonny?"

Lem nudged me to keep talking. "We, uh, we want to make inquiries about a man named Davy Shaw, sir."

"Inquiries, eh? What kind of inquiries?"

"We just want to know where he is and how to get there!" Lem blurted out.

The man took out his cigar and blew smoke into Lem's face. "Well, maybe he doesn't want to be found. Ever think of that? Are you relatives of his?"

"In a way, sir," I stammered. "He and our pa were great friends once."

Before the man in the striped suit could reply, another man in work clothes joined us on the sidewalk. "Newton, what's the holdup? Mr. Hawthorne expects you inside."

"I'm comin'. These boys want Davy Shaw. They say their pa was a friend of his."

The new man turned to us. "Who's your pa, son?" He had a much friendlier face than the cigar-smoking man, so I decided to take a chance.

"Calton Soames, sir," I said.

The new man looked shocked. "Calton Soames? Why, I haven't heard that name in years. You boys are his sons?"

"Yes, sir," piped up Lem.

"Well, come in. There are folks here who will want to see you, for sure." The new man ushered us through the door of the building. The man in the striped suit followed behind us, looking as perplexed as I felt.

The building may have looked dingy on the outside, but the inside was a different story. The walls were paneled three-quarters of the way up in a dark brown wood with forest green wallpaper above. Comfy-looking leather chairs and couches were scattered in groups down the halls, with tables and spittoons handy. Large vases of green plants stood at corners and on tables, and everywhere I looked there were paintings of horses.

The man led us into a spacious room where dozens of men were sitting at tables. Some were drinking coffee, and some were signing papers. A large man, who was also in a striped suit, presided over the room at a huge desk in the front. The wall behind him was lined with glass-front cases from floor to ceiling filled with photographs, medals and trophies. Bronze, silver and gold gleamed from each case, but I didn't have time to look closely. We were urged forward until we were standing in front of the desk before the big man. The room had gone silent as we walked in, and I felt all eyes on our backs as we stood there uncertainly. I brushed against Lem's hand at my side and instantly felt more confident.

"What's this, Hank? Have our pickings gotten so slim, then?" The big man's voice boomed through the room and was met with a smattering of polite laughter.

"Mr. Hawthorne, these boys say they are the sons of Calton Soames."

"Calton Soames, you say? Can it be?" Mr. Hawthorne slapped the desk, stood up and peered at us closely, while several other men gathered round us. "What are your names, boys?"

I swallowed and said, "Dennis is my name, and this is Lemuel." I jerked a thumb at Lem. "We go by Denny and Lem, if you please." I gave a small nudge to Lem to remind him to play along with me pretending to be a boy.

"Nice manners, don't you think, Hank? Their mother probably taught them that. What is your mother's name, son?"

"Lillian Soames, sir," I said proudly. I didn't understand what was happening, but the men didn't seem to be angry. One of them shook Lem's hand, and another one patted me on the back.

Mr. Hawthorne stroked his double chin thoughtfully. "Ah yes, Lillian. She was such a pretty little thing. Just about broke her daddy's heart when she eloped with old Cal." He chuckled. "That Cal sure was something, wasn't he, gents? Always laughing and joking. He liked to play practical jokes on some of you fellows, if I remember right."

Mr. Hawthorne looked sharply at us. "Hey now, he isn't dead, is he?"

"No, sir," said Lem, quickly.

"Good, good. What is your daddy doing these days?"

I rushed to speak before Lem got a word out. "Pap's up in Chicago for some big-time business. We're not exactly sure what kind, but he's doin' real well." Lem looked at me in surprise, and I felt the same. I didn't know what impulse had made me tell that fib, but something deep inside me wanted to protect Pap even when I didn't like him much.

"Big-time business, eh? Why, that's fine."

Another man pushed roughly through the circle of faces around us.

"Look here, Hawthorne. Why all this fuss about Soames? Sure, he just about broke every record possible, but in the end the bad came out in him. You can't forget that he killed the young…"

"Harvey Baker! These are his *children*. We haven't spoken of that tragic accident in the years since it happened, and we will not speak of it now."

The two men bickered back and forth, and I lost track of all they were saying. My mind was reeling. These men were speaking about Pap, a Pap we had never known. A space opened next to Mr. Hawthorne, and I focused on the trophy case behind him. One, two, three, no…four trophies had the name *Calton Soames* engraved on them. I shifted my gaze among the shelves and saw his name several more times, along with photographs of a younger Pap standing next to horses and jockeys, beaming into the camera. So he had been good at working with horses, maybe better than good. But what was this Mr. Baker talking about? Had he really called Pap a killer? I looked at Lem and saw from his confused face that he was thinking the same. I pointed my chin at the trophy case so he'd see Pap's name there too.

My attention returned to the men when Mr. Baker said loudly, "I've said my piece," and pushed back through the circle of men. Mr. Hawthorne turned to us.

"Well now, boys. So what can we do for you?"

I cleared my throat and spoke up. "We want to speak with Davy Shaw, sir. Can you tell us where we can find him?"

"Certainly, I can. Old Davy's the stable manager at Rutledge Farms. What might you want with Davy?"

I hesitated. On the one hand, we were with the folks who could make Lem a jockey, but on the other hand, I had pretended that we were well off. It wouldn't make sense now if I told them we needed work. "We have a message from our pa for Mr. Shaw," I said instead. "Could you give us directions to Rutledge Farms please?"

"Mr. Hawthorne," called out the man named Hank. "I'm heading out Versailles Road to see Don Jessup. I can give the boys a lift. Rutledge is right on the way."

Mr. Hawthorne clapped his hands together. "Alrighty. That'll work out fine." He shook hands with me and then with Lem. "It's been a pleasure to meet you boys. You tell your pa Josiah Hawthorne and the Breeders' Syndicate would be glad for him to visit next time he's in town."

"Thank you, sir," I said, and Lem nodded.

Hank placed his hands on our shoulders and steered us out of the room. As we passed a table laden with breakfast food and coffee, he must have seen us eyeing the food because he told us to take what we wanted while he went to get the keys to his truck. I laid out two napkins and filled each with sausages and biscuits, fruit and one pastry each. I knew when food was scarce that eating sweets just made a body hungrier. We wrapped up the food and stowed it away just as Hank returned.

He noticed our empty hands. "Did you two get some vittles?"

I patted my pack. "Yes, indeed, sir. Thank you kindly. And thank you for the ride."

"No problem at all. Hope you don't mind the back."

"Oh no, sir," said Lem. "That'll be just fine."

We went out the back of the building, and Hank nodded toward an old green truck. Lem climbed up and over the tailgate a bit awkwardly due to his hurt ankle and then offered a hand to pull me up. We settled down facing away from the driver as Hank got in the truck, started the engine and pulled away.

It had been hours since we had eaten, so as soon as the truck was moving, we opened our packs and took out the sausage biscuits and pastries. Having a picnic in the back of a moving truck was a might strange, but we were so hungry that it didn't matter much.

I felt optimistic again. When we were on the train, I'd been keyed up, worried those men wouldn't mind Mr. Red after all and that Shorty would come back for that kiss he wanted. I had never kissed anyone before, and I didn't want that awful, foul-smelling man to take my first kiss from me. Or worse. I closed my mind to thinking what that worse could have been. I sent a silent prayer of thanks upward for Mr. Red and for Hank and Mr. Hawthorne, who had all helped us. It was a good omen that these nice strangers had come our way, and now we would soon meet Davy Shaw and Lem's dream would come true.

Lem interrupted my happy thoughts. With the wind whistling around us, he leaned close to my ear and said, "Dessie, that man who back talked Mr. Hawthorne—he said that Pap killed somebody. Do you believe it?"

I started to deny the possibility. Even though Lem was older by two years, I had always tried to protect him from the harsher side of our lives, as much as I could anyway. But we were on our own now, and he had trusted me enough to come along. Lem deserved honesty, so I said, "I don't know what to believe. You saw the trophies and awards back there with Pap's name all over them. He really was a big-shot horse trainer before we were born. Somethin' made him give that up, and that somethin' must have been bad, but Pap a killer? I just don't know."

Lem finished his lunch and scooted close so we could talk easier. "Pap gets real angry sometimes, and he did hit you the once, but I don't think he's a bad man down at heart. A person would have to be really rotten inside to kill another person. At least that's what I think."

I smiled at him. "Yeah, as mad as I've been at Pap, I don't think he'd hurt somebody on purpose. He just flies off the handle, especially when he's soaked in moonshine." I remembered the words Pap had said to Mam in the night when I wasn't supposed to hear. He'd said that his name would always be linked with something bad that had happened. "But Lem, what if he was drinkin' and he accidentally killed somebody? I could believe that."

My brother nodded. "And then he felt so bad about it that he just couldn't stay around here. I bet you're right, Dess."

"Well, Davy Shaw'll probably know, but let's don't ask him right away, okay? I think we should get to know him first."

"You always have such good ideas." Lem gave me a swift sideways hug. "Say, I've been meanin' to ask. What good news did you have to share the other night?"

"What? Oh, it wasn't important."

"You seemed pretty excited for somethin' that wasn't important." Lem gave me a nudge.

"Oh, all right." I dug into the pocket of my jacket and took out the wadded-up letter Miss Morrissey had given me. "Read this."

Lem looked at me curiously as he flattened the letter. We bent over it so the wind wouldn't carry it away.

"Hey, Dess, this is great! You won a poetry contest for the whole state! You should have told me." Lem's beaming smile meant the world to me, and I couldn't help grinning back. "Tell me your poem."

"Here, in the back of a truck?"

"Sure, why not? Unless you can't remember what you wrote, of course," he teased.

I narrowed my eyes at him. "I remember it. Okay, uhm, it's called 'My Blue Kentucky.'" I cleared my throat, closed my eyes, and recited my poem.

"They say the grass is so green in Kentucky

That it's blue.

They say the meadows are rolling and the horses grow strong

eating bluegrass.

But here in coal mine country we know the truth.

The mine gate opens and along with the men

Who come pouring out hungry and tired,

Comes the dust, silently, silently

Covering the houses, the people, the cars, the grass.

Early in the morning when the dew and the coal dust mingle,

The dust settles in, smothering even the tiniest flutter of life,

And the grass turns a lovely shade of blue."

When I opened my eyes, Lem was looking at me with such a prideful face that I almost started to cry. He took my hand and gave it a squeeze. "That's one fine poem," is all he said, but the moment felt better and bigger than any prize could.

Lem squinted at the letter again. "This says that you have a paid trip for two to the Kentucky Derby in May in Louisville so you can hear your poem read to the crowd by the lieutenant governor before the big race. Dess, you've got to go!"

"No, what I've got to do is get us settled in jobs with Mr. Davy Shaw."

"But hearing your own poem read at the Derby. Gee, it'll probably even be on the radio. Wouldn't the folks back in Whitburn bust with pride to hear it?"

"Well," I conceded, "it might be nice to hear my poem on the radio, but we've got other things to think about right now."

"If we get settled with Mr. Shaw and he likes our work, come May we'll try to get you to the Derby. Deal?"

He held out his hand, and I laughed as we shook on it. I took the crumpled letter and folded it carefully this time before putting it back in my pocket.

The truck was slowing down. It turned off a wide main road onto a curving gravel drive lined with white fences on both sides. A few horses were in the meadows, and a couple of them stopped their grazing to glance in our direction as we passed by. I realized that we'd been so distracted by eating and talking that I hadn't paid any attention to how long it had taken Hank to get to Rutledge Farms. I guessed that wouldn't matter, though, since we would be staying here very soon.

Chapter Nine

Hank drove past several barns and outbuildings before coming to a stop in a dusty clearing between two larger, similar structures. Lem repacked our knapsacks while I tucked my hair up under my cap. Hank stopped the truck but made no move to get out, so we jumped down and went around to the driver's side door.

Hank nodded in the direction of a bald and burly man walking toward us. His right cheek bulged with a wad of tobacco.

"That's Silas Dimkins. He's the trainer here at Rutledge, which makes him second in command under Davy Shaw. He'll get you boys fixed up."

The man scowled as he looked over Lem and me, but he greeted Hank with a smile and a handshake. "Howdy, Hank. What brings you out this way?"

"Afternoon, Silas. I'm on my way to Jessup's, but I stopped to drop off these two."

"Surely Mr. Hawthorne doesn't think Rutledge needs to raid nursery schools for stable hands, does he?" Silas Dimkins laughed heartily at his own joke while we stood awkwardly by. I wished Mr. Shaw would show up soon.

"These boys have private business with Davy, and I know you'll take good care of them." Hank started the truck and turned to us. "Good luck, boys. It was nice to meet you, and like Mr. Hawthorne said, if Calton is ever this way, we'd be glad to see him."

"Thank you again, sir," I said, and Lem echoed me. Hank backed up the truck and headed down the drive. For some reason, I had an urge to yell to him to come back, but that was a childish thought, so I pushed it away and turned to Mr. Dimkins.

He did not look friendly. The smile and hearty manner were gone. He stood with his legs planted apart and his beefy arms crossed over his protruding stomach.

"What's this about business with Davy?" he growled at us around the wad of tobacco in his mouth.

"Uhm, please sir, we'd like to speak with Mr. Shaw," I ventured and tried a smile of my own.

"Mr. Shaw is a busy man, and so am I, for that matter. Two kids can't just ride up in one of Hawthorne's trucks and demand to see the boss man." He jabbed a thumb at himself. "I'm Mr. Shaw's right hand, so if you want to see him, you got to go through me. Now, what is this about?"

Lem decided he should try to charm Mr. Dimkins. Lem could usually charm a polecat out of its stink, but apparently Mr. Dimkins was one mean polecat.

Lem took off his hat and offered a slight bow. "Of course we know how busy you and Mr. Shaw must be, sir. My s…brother and I will be glad to wait. It's just that we've come a long way, you see, to deliver a message from our father, who was a close friend of Mr. Shaw's. Perhaps you could show us a place we could sit until Mr. Shaw has time for us. We'd be right grateful."

Mr. Dimkins's sour expression didn't change. He studied us in silence as he worked his gums, chewing the tobacco. We jumped back as he spit a stream of dark brown juice toward us.

"Can't do that. Mr. Shaw ain't here. Not sure when he'll be back. So you two need to move along."

"Please, Mr. Dimkins, can you tell us where he's gone?" I pleaded.

"Nope," said the man over his shoulder as he walked away. As he headed toward a paddock down the lane, he bawled out orders to a group of men gathered there, but I didn't understand the words.

My brother and I looked at each other helplessly. I felt tears prick behind my eyes, but I knew if I started crying, I'd have a hard time continuing my disguise as a boy. We started shuffling slowly back down the lane. I tried to come up with an idea of what to do next, but my mind was a blank. I didn't understand. Hank and Mr. Hawthorne sure thought Davy Shaw was at Rutledge Farms. I wondered if maybe Mr. Dimkins lied to us, but why would he have done that? We were complete strangers to him.

As we were passing the edge of the building, we heard a *pssst* sound. I looked over, and a skinny man in overalls was beckoning to us. I looked at Lem, and he shrugged his shoulders, so we hurried over and followed the man around behind the building where he led us.

"Old Silas didn't tell you the truth," the man whispered. "Davy's gone to Churchill, but he'll be back in three days. And I think he'd want to see you boys."

"Oh mister, thank you for telling us. We'll try to come back on…let's see, on Monday. Can you get us in to see Mr. Shaw?"

The man looked aghast at my question. "Oh no, sonny. I've said too much now, but it just boiled my blood to hear him lyin' to you. If you come back, don't let Silas know it was me who told, okay?" He looked around furtively. "Now you boys better go."

I turned to Lem. "Three days is all. We can wait three days." He nodded.

I turned back to thank the man, but he'd disappeared already.

"I guess that Mr. Dimkins has everybody around here scared," I said.

We made our way back to the lane with our moods brighter and our steps lighter than they'd been a few moments before. The thought popped in my head that we'd been helped by another good Samaritan. That was four so far. I wondered if we'd reached our limit.

Our course down the lane took us by the crowd of men at the paddock. Silas Dimkins had pushed to the front and was leaning over the fence. He never turned around to look our way, as his attention was fixed on the scene in the center of the fenced-in circle of ground. Two men held ropes attached to the bridle of a horse. And what a horse! Even as someone who didn't know much about horses, I could see this one was a beauty. The horse was coal black with a coat that shimmered in the sun. His mane was thick and inky black. His well-chiseled head towered above the men, but his eyes were wild. He snorted fiercely and stomped around, trying to shed the ropes that held him.

Lem stopped walking and stood transfixed, staring at the horse. "Oh, she's a rare one, she is," he whispered. "At least sixteen hands. And look at those strong legs. That's where Thoroughbreds get their speed, you see." His hands curled reflexively, as though he was holding reins atop the horse I now knew was a filly, not a gelding.

As we watched, Silas Dimkins pushed a third man through the paddock gate. "Your turn, Bob. Let's see if you can do any better," he growled.

The man looked frightened but then began to swagger. "I'll show this little lady who's boss, Mr. Dimkins," he called.

At my side, Lem breathed, "Oh no, not that way."

The man checked his spurs and hitched up his pants. The horse was now standing quietly, her head and eyes cast down. I noticed that she had a perfectly formed five-pointed star on her forehead between her eyes. The man called Bob grabbed hold of the pommel, put one foot in a stirrup and swung into the saddle. The horse barely twitched.

Bob grabbed the reins and kicked the horse's sides to get her to move. I winced as the spurs bit into that shiny coat, but the horse responded, walking slowly in a circle around the paddock. Mr. Dimkins spat out a stream of tobacco and nodded while the men around him cheered. Bob brought the horse back to stand in front of the group. He nodded to the other men and took one hand off the reins to raise his hat in celebration of his achievement.

Lem grabbed my arm. "Here she goes, Dess."

He was right, of course. The horse looked up, and I could have sworn she looked right at us. Then she was off, bucking and whinnying across the paddock while Bob bounced up and down and tried in vain to grab the reins in both hands. He dug the spurs in again and slapped at the horse's side with his hat, but in only a few seconds, she sent him flying through the air to land in a heap in front of Mr. Dimkins.

Lem started to run toward the paddock, and in an instant, I knew he intended to confront those men about how they were treating the horse. I stuck out a foot and tripped him. Lem sprawled in the gravel. He was hopping mad himself and knocked my arm away when I bent down to help him up. I didn't care.

"Don't be a fool, Lem," I hissed. "You can't go tellin' off those men. We need to come back here and meet Davy Shaw in three days. If you get us thrown out, we won't be able to do that."

He got up slowly and glared at me but started limping down the lane. I guessed that fall hadn't helped his already hurt ankle any. Lem had left his pack in the rocks. I picked it up and carried both bundles as I caught up with him. We walked in silence to the end of the driveway, and then with a mutual shrug, we turned toward town.

***

Progress was slow. Two hours later, we were still outside town, and the sun was going down. I had hoped we would be able to spend the night in a church shelter, but I could see that wasn't going to happen. Besides, Lem's pain had gotten worse as we'd walked. He hadn't complained, of course, but his steps were slow and labored.

"Look, Lem. There's a barn in that field. You rest a bit, and I'll go check it out. Maybe we can stay the night there."

"Okay, Dess," he said through gritted teeth.

I dropped both bundles next to Lem, climbed over the short fence and loped through the field. Even though I knew we were in dire straits, with food running out and no money, I felt irrationally happy. The land was lovely here, with rolling hills and clear, clean air. I sure didn't miss the coal dust and the constant haze of Whitburn. I lifted my face to the setting sun and smiled at the warmth of its last rays.

When I reached the barn, I sneaked around it, listening for sounds of people. I didn't hear any, even when I opened the barn door slowly and ducked quickly inside. I crept through the barn until I felt sure I was alone. I saw a ladder to a hayloft and was about to climb it when someone nudged me from behind.

I shrieked and spun around to face the farmer, searching for an excuse to offer.

A wide face with soft brown eyes looked at me. I laughed in relief. "Hey there, Bessie." I patted the cow, and she gave a low but friendly moo. "You won't mind sharin' your warm home with us, will you?" I asked.

I quickly returned to Lem and helped him climb over the fence and walk to the barn. I introduced him to Bessie, and he delightedly scratched her behind the ears and fed her some hay while I took our bundles up to the loft.

"Lem, this'll be fine."

I headed back down the ladder and helped Lem climb up. We spread our extra clothes on the hay and settled down.

"Let me see that ankle," I said. I unwrapped the bandage and was dismayed to see how swollen it was. I decided he should sleep with it unbound. I made a makeshift pillow from hay and rags so he could prop his leg.

He lay back and closed his eyes. I looked for a while at his tired face and noticed the blue smudges under his eyes. I knew he was hurting more than he'd ever let on.

While Lem rested, I rummaged through the barn. I found a bucket and took it outside to the well. I cleaned out the bucket and half-filled it with water. I did a quick splash myself to clean my face and hands. I took the water up to Lem and got out the last of our biscuits and an apple. We ate in tired silence and washed the food down with sips of water.

I told Lem to put his ankle in the bucket of cold water, thinking that might reduce the swelling. He jumped a bit at the chill but kept his foot in the water.

"This is just right, Dessie, thank you," said Lem with a sigh.

"Well, it's not quite what I'd planned, but it'll do."

Lem smiled even though his eyes were closed. "My sister, the planner. So what's the plan for the next three days?"

"I've been thinkin' about that, of course. I heard some of those men in the line talkin' today. They said there was a soup kitchen at the corner of Broadway and Vine Streets and a church a few blocks beyond where folks who are down on their luck can get a bed. If we start out walkin' early again tomorrow, we should be able to get a hot meal for lunch and then go over to the church. Maybe we can stay there until Monday."

Lem opened one bright blue eye. "And what happens then?"

"Then we go back to the Breeders' office and see if Hank can give us another lift to Rutledge to see Davy Shaw."

"You think he'll do that a second time?"

"He seemed awfully nice, and if he won't do it, I'll ask Mr. Hawthorne."

Lem lay back again and closed his eyes. "Okay, Dessie. We'll do all that...tomorrow." His breathing became slow and even, and I knew he was asleep. Gently, I pulled his foot out of the bucket of water, dried it off and put his sock back on.

Even though we were out of the night air, the barn started to get chilly. I wished I had brought real blankets with us rather than just the rags I'd used to tie up the bundles. But they were better than nothing, so I snuggled close to Lem and pulled them over us.

When I woke the next morning, I immediately knew something was wrong. Lem wasn't next to me. "Lem, where are you?"

"Down here, sleepyhead," a voice called.

I looked over the edge of the hayloft, but I didn't see him. Bessie was below, though, calmly chewing hay. "Where are you?"

His face peeked out over the cow's back. "Right here. Come on down. I have a surprise for you."

I took the time to tie up our rag bundles and spread hay back over where we had lain before heading down the ladder. I came around the back of the cow and was hit in the face by a spray of warm milk!

"Hey, what's the big idea?"

Lem grinned. "Breakfast is the idea, silly." He turned the cow's teat he was grasping in his own direction and squirted a stream into his mouth. "Oh, that's good," he said. "Your turn."

I was so glad to see Lem back to himself that I dutifully opened my mouth and let him squirt milk into it. He was right; the milk was warm and sweet. We took turns taking mouthfuls as the cow stood placidly by. We were giggling so loudly at each other that we didn't hear the farmer until he was right behind us.

"What in tarnation do you think you're doing?" a voice bellowed. We both jumped, and Lem's fingers slipped, sending sticky milk spraying down my shirt.

"You young hoodlums owe me for that milk and, I wager, for a night spent in my barn!" The man towered over us, his face flushed and angry.

"We...we're sorry, sir. We didn't have anywhere to go, you see, and we were cold and hungry..."

"Just stow that sob story, boy. Everybody has it hard these days. Now, you pay me for the milk or I take payment out of your hides. What's your choice?"

The farmer grabbed a hayfork from the barn wall. He was between us and the door. I couldn't think of anything to do, but Lem spoke up.

"Of course you know we don't have any money, sir, but we can work. My brother and I can do chores for you to pay for the milk. I'll just keep milkin', and Denny can go collect the eggs and feed the chickens. Does that seem like a fair trade to you, sir?"

Lem's open face and winning ways worked their usual magic. The farmer hesitated and lowered the hayfork. "I'll make that deal. But I want you boys to weed the vegetable garden too."

"We'll be glad to do that, mister, but only if you feed us some breakfast." I found my voice after all. Lem rolled his eyes at me to say he thought I had gone too far.

The farmer's stern expression changed, and he chuckled. "Well, all right, then. I'll rustle up some eggs and bread for you. Now get started on the chores." He left the barn.

I peeked out the door and saw him walking toward his farmhouse. "Okay, Lem, now's our chance. Let's go."

"Go, Dessie? We're not going anywhere. At least not until we've finished the chores."

I looked at him in disbelief. "You mean you meant that? I thought it was just a trick to buy us some time to get away."

"No, the farmer was right. Drinkin' that milk was stealin'. We may be on our own, but we ain't thieves. At least not yet." Lem sat down again on the milking stool and patted Bessie. I soon heard the milk streaming into the pail.

"Oh, you and your high morals," I sighed. "I guess I should have told that farmer that I like my eggs over easy!" I grabbed a basket and headed to the chicken coop.

***

The farmer, who told us his name was Turnball, brought us each one fried egg and one piece of toast. We could have eaten three times that, but we thanked him profusely all the same. Lem showed him the pails of milk Bessie had produced, and I proudly displayed two baskets of eggs I had wrestled from squawking, pecking chickens. If there was a trick to taking eggs from hens, I sure didn't know it, but I had prevailed, and the farmer seemed pleased.

After breakfast, we weeded the garden, which turned out to be about as twice as large as the word *garden* had conjured up in my mind. Lem's ankle was better, but I made him take lots of breaks to rest it. Farmer Turnball checked our work frequently and fretted over every tiny weed, so it was mid-morning before he finally shook hands with Lem that our deal was done and we could get on our way.

As we walked, I asked Lem about the horse we'd seen at Rutledge Farms the day before.

"I'm sorry I had to trip you yesterday. Why were you upset at those men?"

"They call it breakin'. A rider tries to force a horse that's new to a bridle and saddle to submit to the rider's will. It just don't make sense to me to do it that way. If you put yourself in the place of the horse, would you want to be held by ropes or forced to carry someone around on your back all of a sudden when you've always run free? Seems to me that a horse should be a rider's partner and friend, and that's no way to treat a friend."

"How would you train a horse then?"

"I'd spend lots of time with the horse so he'd get used to me and talk real calm and quiet to him. I'd introduce him, slow-like, you know, to the bridle. And I'd start by tryin' to ride him bareback before I ever would put a saddle on."

"You've thought a lot about this, haven't you?"

"Well, sure. When I was in the mine, I had to have somethin' to think about. You had told me my dreams would come true, so I thought about that when I was feelin' low." Lem hooked his arm in mine. "Dessie, I'm glad you kidnapped me two nights ago. Even if it doesn't work out in the end, I wouldn't have missed this adventure."

"That's good, but don't go borrowin' trouble, as Mother Gumbs would say. It'll all work out fine; you'll see." I said this as much to buck myself up as to encourage my brother. I wasn't sure what we'd find in Lexington.

Chapter Ten

We reached the Vine Street soup kitchen in mid-afternoon, well past lunchtime and too early for supper. Exhausted and starving, we dragged ourselves up to the converted storefront. I reached to push open the door and banged into it.

Lem solemnly pointed to the closed sign that I had missed. Under it hung another sign that listed the hours. It served only breakfast and lunch on Saturdays and was closed on Sundays, so there was no point in waiting around for the supper hour.

We sat dejectedly down on the stoop. I put my chin in my hand and tried to decide what we should do next.

"I'm so sorry. I had no idea it'd be closed."

"No, it's my fault. If I hadn't milked that cow and offered to do chores for Farmer Turnball, we'd have made it in time."

I patted his arm lethargically. "Well, we've missed a meal before."

"What should we do now, Dess?"

"I think we should go find the First Christian Church and see about a place to sleep. I heard a man say it was a couple of blocks from the center of town, so it shouldn't be too far from here."

"Okay with me. I guess we can just walk around lookin' up for steeples."

I smiled at his thin joke as we stood up. It turned out that the center of town was only two streets away. We came upon it rather suddenly. We turned a corner and almost got knocked down by the crowds bustling up and down the sidewalks.

A small park stood across the street from a five-story domed courthouse. Even if I hadn't been able to guess what the building was, the two flagpoles out front clearly identified it. The U.S. flag and the blue Kentucky flag danced in the cool breeze. The street was lined with cars and trucks of all shapes and sizes. Some of the trucks were parked haphazardly near the park, their tailgates open. The truck beds spilled wares the farmers and their wives had brought to sell and trade.

Since it was Saturday, we were in the midst of market day. Housewives in cotton dresses rushed from store to store, towing along weary, distracted children. I took Lem's elbow and steered him close to the sides of the buildings so we could navigate our way without danger of being knocked into the way of the electric street trolley. We watched the trolley as it whizzed up and down the street, clanging its bell to signify an upcoming stop. Whenever it paused and a dozen or so people jumped off, another dozen jumped on. Lem nodded toward it, wanting to take a ride, but I shook my head, knowing we couldn't spare any coins. That rat-fink Brendan Cole had left us only our pocket change, and I was determined to make the dollar and sixty-nine cents last as long as possible.

I thought of Mam back in Whitburn, slowly walking up and down the same aisles, hoping to spy something new. She would have loved it here, where every store offered different goods, many that we had never seen before. We stopped to look at a display of unusual vegetables outside a grocer's. But since my stomach was rumbling, I wouldn't have passed up trying any food right then, no matter how strange.

We took our time looking in shop windows and browsing through some of the stores. As bustling as the city seemed, I noticed that many of the ladies' carts contained only a few items and that many store shelves seemed bare. I realized that even a town as large as Lexington was being hurt by the Depression.

In the next block, the stores were nicer, with fancier signs and curtains that drew back to show off carefully laid window displays. We passed a store that sold only ladies' hats and another that sold only little girls' dresses. My attention was caught by a flash of shiny light. When I drew near the window, I realized it was a jewelry store. The display showed watches, rings, bracelets and necklaces of all shapes and sizes. Gold, silver and sparkling jewels winked in the afternoon sun. I craned my neck to gaze into the shop through the window and found what I was looking for—a small case of jeweled brooches. I fingered the horse brooch pinned to the inside of my jacket and wondered if I should take it inside and try to sell it.

"Lem, wait while I go in this store, okay?"

His eyes grew round as he realized what type of store it was, but he dutifully sat down on the curb to wait for me, content to look around.

I sidled into the store and turned my head down as though I was looking through the nearest case but peered upward through my eyelashes. A young woman, an older woman and a middle-aged man stood behind the counters. I figured the man was the one to talk to and edged myself behind a boy about Lem's age who had just stepped up to speak to the jeweler.

The boy pulled a diamond ring out of his pocket and held it out.

"Please, sir, I would like to sell this ring."

The jeweler put a strange-looking glass up to his eye and carefully examined the ring. "Nice quality diamond. Where did you get this, son?" he asked, smiling.

"M-m-my mother," stammered the boy. His neck turned red, and the color spread upward to his cheeks.

The man kept the pleasant look on his face. "And where is your mother? Why hasn't she brought it in to sell herself?"

"She's s-s-sick. We need the m-m-money to pay the doctor. Please, I'll take half wh-what it's worth." The boy fidgeted with the cap in his hand.

"I bet you would take half," sneered the jeweler, all friendliness gone. "This ring is stolen, boy! No petty crook can trick me into buying stolen jewelry."

"I swear it's my mother's!" The boy grabbed the ring back and rushed by me, knocking me into a display case of watches.

"Thief! Stop him!" the man yelled, his face purpling with rage. None of the surprised customers did as he bid. In frustration, he fumbled to get around the young shop assistant, and by the time he made his way out the door, the boy was long gone. I pushed myself to my feet, cursing the luck that had put the boy in the shop just ahead of me. Now the jeweler would never believe that the brooch I had to sell had belonged to my mother either. The only way I would ever be able to sell the jewels was if I had an adult to vouch for me.

The jeweler came back in the store, cursing under his breath. As I tried to walk past, he grabbed me by the collar and pulled me up to stare in my face.

"Were you with that boy? Are you his partner?" he demanded as the other customers stepped away.

"No! No, sir." I thrust my right hand instinctively into my pocket and closed my fingers around the hilt of the knife, but I knew I shouldn't pull it out here. Then I spied Lem waiting patiently on the curb and pointed to him instead. "There's my brother. He's waiting for me."

Time seemed to stop as the man looked at me for another long moment before he relaxed his hold on my jacket. "Well, did you want something?"

"I…I thought I saw a chain for my father's watch, but it won't do." I tipped my cap at the jeweler and pulled it down over my eyes. "Thankee kindly and good day."

I called to Lem as I left the shop, and we walked slowly but steadily away. When we reached the next corner, I turned sharply. I started to run and tugged on Lem's arm to follow me. I glanced at him and was relieved to see that he was able to run now without limping. We bolted down the block, dodging in and out of startled shoppers, and turned at the next corner away from the center of town. I strained my ears for police whistles behind us, but it seemed we were in the clear.

I stopped at a bench, and Lem plopped down beside me. "You didn't rob that store, did you?" he asked between deep breaths.

I wriggled my nose at him. "No, but the shop owner thought the boy ahead of me was trying to sell a stolen ring and that I was his partner."

"Oh…why did you go in that store, Dess? We don't have any money."

As I gazed into Lem's trusting blue eyes, I decided it was time to tell him about Mam and Pap's other secret. If he was going to run the risk of being chased by angry storekeepers and possibly police, he had a right to know.

"Lem, I brought a little insurance along with us; at least I thought it would be something we could break apart and sell if we needed money, but now I'm not so sure." I scooted closer to my brother and checked to see if anyone was looking our way. I opened my jacket a bit so he could see the horse brooch.

"Where did you get that?!"

"It was Mam's."

"I've never seen it before." Lem ran his hand through his hair, a gesture I've seen him do countless times when he's thinking hard.

"That's because it was hidden, along with a bunch of other jewelry. I overheard Mam and Pap talking about their hidden treasure, and I thought it was money, but when I went to dig it up, all I found was jewelry."

Lem frowned. "You shouldn't have taken it, Dessie."

"I know, but I was disappointed there was no money, and I was mad, Lem. Pap and Mam could sell some of those jewels and pay back on the old house, but Pap won't do it. He'd rather see you stuck in the mine before your time for a fire that was his fault in the first place."

"So you took it and we came here, but now you can't sell it because that man will think you stole it."

"Yes," I said dejectedly and slumped against him. "I've messed everythin' up."

Lem patted my back. "Well, not everythin'," he said. "Look yonder, there's a steeple. That could be the church with the shelter."

Seeing that steeple lifted my spirits, and we got up and walked toward it. The First Christian Church was a block away, situated on a corner. There was no one in sight on the street we were on, and I laughed in relief, feeling it was a good sign that they would have room for us. But my relief was short-lived. When we turned the corner, we found a line stretching two blocks long of men, women and children waiting for the doors to open.

As we passed the line to reach the end, I silently cursed myself for the time we had wasted looking at shops and being distracted by the jewelry incident. We could have been in that line an hour or two before if I'd only been careful and had thought ahead.

As it was, we sat and stood in line for another two hours and watched silently as dozens more bedraggled people lined up behind us. Unlike the line at the Breeders' Syndicate where the men had shared tips and stories, the people in this line didn't speak much. The silence was broken only by coughing or the whining of little children. While we waited, I vowed to myself that once we were working for Davy Shaw, I'd never stand in another line for a handout again. I wanted to curse Brendan Cole again, but I didn't have the energy. I was finding that being broke and hungry was exhausting as well as frightening.

A lady with a large cross hanging around her neck finally opened the doors, and people filed slowly into the church's annex building. As we got closer, I became anxious when I saw the lady asking people questions and writing on a clipboard before they were admitted. A few people were even turned away.

Finally, we were next. The lady looked us over and asked, "Are you boys alone?"

"Yes'm," I said, squaring my shoulders.

"And where are your parents?" she asked gently.

"Pap went to heaven, and Mam sent us to find jobs in the city so we can send money back to her and the little ones," I stated. I didn't like telling lies, but I was still afraid of letting too many folks know who we really were.

The lady smiled, and her eyes were kind. "I'm so sorry for your loss. I don't know that we can help you boys, though." She gestured down at her clipboard. "I'm afraid we only have two beds left for tonight: one in the men's ward and one in the women's."

This was a problem I hadn't anticipated. Lem lifted his eyebrows at me, wondering what I would do. Stupid me had assumed we'd have a room to ourselves, like in the hotels we heard about. But this wasn't a hotel, and of course they'd be packing lots of people in a big room together. I didn't want to be separated from Lem though. I decided not to tell her I was a girl.

"Thank you anyway, ma'am." I touched my cap to her, noting the time the shelter opened the next day on the sign behind her. "Perhaps another time."

The lady smiled kindly and turned to the couple standing behind us. They wouldn't turn down food and a bed, as I had just done.

I could feel Lem worrying in the slight tremor of his hand on my arm as we walked away, but he didn't complain. He trusted me to find us somewhere to stay the night. I wasn't sure I trusted me though.

I knew we could head toward the poor part of the city and probably find a camp or two of other destitute souls, but my mind went back to the man in the boxcar called Shorty, and I knew I didn't want to take a chance on running up against other men like him with no Mr. Red to protect us.

In the middle of the next block, I spied an alley and took a chance that it would lead to what I wanted. The alley opened onto a quiet street of big, lovely houses. My heart lifted. There were places to hide on this street, and no one was about. We crossed the lawn of a large gray house and sneaked around to the back. One more house over and I found it.

We climbed up the rope ladder to some lucky child's tree house and then pulled the ladder after us. We sat down on the wooden plank floor and waited for our breathing to slow and our hearts to go back to beating at normal speed.

There was no heat here, of course, and we couldn't start a fire, but at least we were hidden from the world and out of the night wind. I unpacked our bundles and laid out what was left of the food. We had four chunks of bread, four apples and a wedge of cheese. I set aside two apples, divided the cheese in half and repacked the remaining bread and fruit. As we ate our dinner half-asleep with exhaustion, I remembered something important.

"Lem," I whispered. "I forgot until now that today's your birthday. You're sixteen."

"That's funny. I had forgotten too."

"I'm sorry this isn't much of a birthday for you."

He smiled faintly. "But it's one I won't forget."

I laid out extra clothes to make a bed of sorts for us, and when Lem lay down, I snuggled in close and pulled the rags up, like I had the night before.

The next morning, we woke cold and stiff in the freezing early dawn. We repacked our bundles and slipped down the rope ladder and out to the sidewalk as quickly as possible. Before falling asleep the night before, I had devised a plan for the day. I told Lem my plan as we walked away from the rich people's houses, and he nodded in agreement, blowing on his fingers to try to warm them.

We retraced our steps from two days before to the train station. As I had hoped, we found an open coffee shop in the station. We took a booth, and I ordered two coffees, handing over precious coins from our meager supply of change. We drank three cups each, loading the coffee with cream and sugar, until the waitress started shooting mean glances our way.

We hung out at the train station for the rest of the morning until it was time to get in line again at the First Christian Church at one o'clock. We were in the first ten people to line up this time. I was determined that we would not spend another night in the cold tree house. After another lengthy wait, the kind lady opened the doors again. This time, she quickly wrote down the false names I gave her and ushered us into the men's ward together.

The men's ward was a large, high-ceilinged room with about three dozen narrow cots lined up in two neat rows. I grabbed Lem's hand and pulled him to an open corner so I could take a cot closest to the wall. We lay down on our cots gratefully and immediately went to sleep. We napped away the afternoon, but Lem woke me in time to shuffle through a line in another large room for soup and a sandwich. Families sat together eating and talking quietly. I directed Lem to another corner, and we ate in silence, only nodding to the folks around us.

I couldn't say what I was feeling out loud because it would have sounded so ungrateful. I appreciated the fact that the good people of the First Christian Church were providing us a bed and food when we were in need, but I also felt that every worker was silently judging us. As poor as our family was in Whitburn, we were no worse off than anyone else there, excepting Mr. Joe and his wife. Mam and Pap had never taken a handout, and we kids had never known at home the kind of hunger we'd felt the past two days. I was angry at the world, but I was also angry at myself. I should have planned more, saved up more, brought more supplies. Mostly, I shouldn't have been so stupid as to believe a handsome stranger.

Lem seemed to understand what I was feeling even though I kept my mouth shut. He reached over in the middle of eating his soup and squeezed my hand. "It's okay, Dess. Don't be so hard on yourself. We'll get a ride to Rutledge Farms, like you said, and find Davy Shaw."

After supper, the lady in charge brought out the radio, and everyone stayed in the dining hall to listen to Rudy Vallee and Eddie Cantor. Then it was back to bed. We took off our shoes and outer clothes, but I told Lem to stow them inside the bed, under the covers. I had heard a rumor when I returned our dishes earlier that some patrons steal items when the others are sleeping. I made sure to sleep on top of the horse brooch that night. Even though it hadn't helped us so far, I wanted to keep it safe.

The following morning, we ate a breakfast of lumpy oatmeal and went on our way. We walked to the Breeders' Syndicate office with the energy that only comes from sleeping in a warm bed. Our sleep had been fitful, though, due to the coughs that came from the man in the bed next to Lem. I had noticed that he didn't get up for breakfast either. I glanced at Lem, looking for signs of illness, but his stride was strong and he was in good spirits.

Those good spirits were dashed minutes later when we stood outside the empty and closed Breeders' office. A sign I hadn't noticed before said it was closed on Mondays.

"What do we do now, Dess?"

"I guess we start walking, Lem. Maybe we can hitch a ride outside town, but even if we can't, we should be able to get to Rutledge by suppertime."

Lem nodded and set us back on the path we had taken before. When we reached the outskirts of town, we stopped at a small stream to rest and get a drink of water. I noticed that Lem was sweating heavily, but he said it was just from walking.

As if to prove that he was feeling fine, Lem started singing coal mining songs as we walked along the road toward the Thoroughbred farm. He had learned the songs in the weeks he'd worked in the mine, as the miners often sang to relieve the boredom of digging and hauling coal.

The song I liked best was called "Coal Dust Blues." Lem taught me the words, and we sang together:

"Down, boys, down we go.

Down to the dark, dark depths below.

Say goodbye to those who are dear.

You may not see them again up here.

I got the Coal Dust Blues, oh yeah.

I got the Coal Dust Blues.

Work, boys, work all night.

Swing that pick and hit that pike.

Fill that bucket with Old Man Coal.

So the old boss man won't sell your soul.

I got the Coal Dust Blues, oh yeah.

I got the Coal Dust Blues."

Lem's voice broke on the last word. He stopped and bent over in a spasm of coughing.

"Lem! You are sick, aren't you?" I felt his slick forehead and found it hot with fever. Lem's face had grown pale, and dark circles had formed under his eyes. I made him sit down by the side of the road and forced him to eat one of the apples that remained since we had no water. He promptly rolled to the side and lost the apple and the oatmeal he had eaten that morning. He lay back with his head on a rag bundle.

"Now I feel better. Just give me a minute to rest and I'll be ready to go again."

I went to the edge of the road to see if I could flag down a car or truck. There were not many on the road, but the ones that did come by ignored my frantic waving.

I heaved a heavy sigh and returned to Lem's side. "Come on, Lem. We have to keep moving."

He tried to stand but immediately lost his balance. I put an arm around his waist and his arm across my shoulder. I carried the two rag bundles in my other hand.

With Lem practically dead on his feet and needing frequent rest breaks, our progress was very slow the rest of the day. In late afternoon, we stopped under the shade of a large magnolia tree, and I stretched my aching shoulder muscles.

"I remember this tree," I said excitedly. "We're not far from Rutledge Farms now. Maybe a mile more is all."

He offered me a wan smile. "Okay, Dessie," he said weakly. "Don't worry. I can make it."

I helped Lem up, and we had just started off again when I heard an ominous sound. Thunder! I prayed the storm would pass us by, but as the sky darkened, I knew it was not to be. When the first bolt of lightning lit the sky, I moved us away from the treeline. We were soaked through in only a few seconds when the rain quickly followed.

We hobbled onward. I could feel Lem shivering uncontrollably, but there was nothing I could do for him except keep walking. The rain on my face mingled with the tears streaming down. Night had fallen by the time I saw the lane leading into Rutledge Farms. I almost sobbed with joy.

"Look, Lem. There's the lane to Rutledge. We're almost there."

Lem's teeth were chattering so that he couldn't answer. He nodded and redoubled his efforts to walk, but his steps were growing even slower and clumsier. I realized I wasn't going to be able to get him all the way to the main stable yard. I spied a stable set back from the lane and decided to take him there.

I opened the gate to the narrow track to the stable and helped Lem through the opening. Together we half walked, half crawled the remaining yards to the stable. Thankfully, when I gave the door a nudge, it opened easily.

It was such a blessing to be out of the rain. The stable was small, and since it was isolated from the main buildings, I first thought it was empty. But as I dragged Lem into an empty stall and lay him down on a pile of hay, a horse whinnied loudly and began banging its hooves against the wall. Lem didn't notice. He had fallen into unconsciousness.

I was at my wit's end. I stormed around the door to the other stall, prepared to yell at the creature making such a racket. My words died in my throat when I realized that I knew this horse.

Chapter Eleven

"You're the black beauty we saw in the paddock three days ago!" I
exclaimed. The horse ignored me. She tossed her head in the air and
continued to whinny and jump around her stall. She was clearly agitated,
but so was I. She could just be angry for all I cared.

I rushed back to check on Lem. He was still unconscious, and his
breathing was labored. I touched the back of my hand to his forehead and
found that he was burning with fever. I sat back on my heels and stared
at his pale, dear face. I felt a panic rising within me until it settled like a
lead weight in my chest. I didn't know what to do, but I had to do
something. He was getting worse every minute.

I closed my eyes and rocked back and forth and tried to think clearly. I
guessed that the stable was a mile or so from the main compound, so if I
walked it in the rain, it would take me at least a half hour. I would have
to leave Lem alone. If he woke up, he wouldn't know where I'd gone. I
looked frantically through our bundles, but there was no paper and no
pencil.

I felt tears starting again and furiously wiped them away. Crying wouldn't help Lem. He'd just have to know that I'd gone for help. If only I could get there faster. If only…

A calm stillness came over me then, and I knew what I would do. As though in a daze, I stood up slowly and walked around to the other stall. As I grabbed a handful of feed from a bucket by the door, I heard Lem's words in my mind from three days before when he talked about how he'd gentle the horse to get her trust. I opened the latch to the stall and held out my hand. I approached the huge beast, my head down but my eyes looking up at her through my lashes.

"There, there, girl. Will you be my friend, you beauty?" I asked in a slow, calm whisper.

The horse stilled, looking at me curiously.

"You are such a good, good girl. Come and have some grain," I whispered. I forced myself to stillness, standing like a statue with hand extended.

The horse approached me slowly. She snorted gently and blew hot air on my neck. It seemed like hours but I guess it was just seconds as she looked me over. She seemed to come to a decision to accept me. She gave a little whinny and bent her great head to my hand. I felt the velvety wetness of her mouth as she ate.

I reached out with my other hand to gently scratch and rub the perfect white star between her eyes. "Can I call you Star?" I asked. "Here's the thing, Star. I need your help. My brother's really sick, and I need to get to the other people as fast as I can. I'm not a good rider like Lem is, but if you'll let me, I'll try to hang on."

I poured all this out to that horse, and she did the strangest thing. She brought her head up and stared in my eyes. Then I swear she nodded and turned her head toward her back, as though inviting me to get on.

I took an empty bucket and turned it over next to Star. I closed my eyes for a second and sent up a wish to my wishing star, wherever it was, then climbed on the bucket and reached for Star's mane. I leaped up and by some miracle found myself on her back, my hands gripping her mane.

She didn't try to buck me off the way I had seen her do to the stable hands the other day. She seemed to sense that we had a mission.

"Okay, girl. Let's go," I said and tugged her mane gently toward the stable door.

Star responded, and we plodded out of the stable. I sent a last look back at Lem, still unconscious.

The rain pelted me in the face like a million tiny needles, and I was instantly drenched. I pushed my heels in Star's flanks with gentle pressure and urged her forward. She started to trot and then to gallop. I tightened my grip on her mane and lay low over her back, holding on as best I could.

It was a wild ride. The night was dark and cold, and the rain poured down in sheets so that I could barely see anything in front of us. The horse moved effortlessly under me, and though I was terrified, I was also exhilarated at being able to ride this powerful creature. Star was in control, not me, and luckily, she knew just where I needed to go. We pounded down the track from the stable to the lane leading to the rest of the farm, and without hesitating, Star turned right and headed toward the main stable yard.

Lem's cap was plastered to my head, but some wet curls escaped and lashed my face, falling in my eyes and blinding me further. I only knew we were getting close to the main buildings when I felt Star begin to slow beneath me.

She pulled to an abrupt stop in the same spot where Hank had parked his truck three days before. As I tried to catch my breath and unlock a hand to wipe hair out of my eyes, she let out a great whinny and then another and another.

Lights went on over the doors to the buildings on either side of the yard. Men stumbled out of the buildings, grumbling as they pulled on rain gear. One voice cut through all the noise.

"What's goin' on here?" growled Silas Dimkins. He suddenly materialized on the ground below me. Star immediately began to fidget and back away. She turned in circles, trying to avoid the grabbing hands of the men surrounding us. One of the men grabbed for Star's bridle but pulled back in surprise when he didn't find one.

"Please, Mr. Dimkins," I called down. "My brother is sick and…"

"Why in tarnation is this horse out of her stable?" He ignored me, but I tried again.

"We met you three days ago, Mr. Dimkins. I need your help!"

I dug my heels into Star's flanks a bit harder to try to keep her in one place. Mr. Dimkins peered up through the rain at me as though seeing me there for the first time. My heart sank as a twisted grin spread across his ugly face. "Well, boys, looks like we've got us a horse thief." He turned his back to me and jerked a thumb over his shoulder, saying, "Pull him down and take that crazy horse back to the stable. Then we'll have some fun dealing with the horse thief."

Before any of the stable hands could react, Star turned in a half circle and thrust a leg backward. Her hoof hit Mr. Dimkins squarely in the back and sent him flying forward to land face down in the mud.

Star reared up and flailed her forelegs at the men surrounding us. They wisely backed away, and she hit the ground running forward, with me still clinging to her back. As we sped away, I heard Silas Dimkins cursing and yelling behind us, so I knew Star hadn't killed him at least.

The horse galloped from the main stable yard on toward the big house at the end of the lane. I gazed at it in wonder through the wet curls hanging over my eyes. Red bricks, white shutters and green ivy covered the huge three-story mansion that was fronted by tall white columns and a deep porch. It was the house I had told Lem about, the house of my dreams.

I didn't have time to ponder long on this though. Lights were already illuminating the circular drive in front of the house, and a small group of men and women had gathered there, a few holding lanterns in their hands. I guessed they were servants of the mansion.

Star galloped into the midst of this group and stopped so abruptly that I almost flew over her head. I sat up and took a deep breath. I needed to interrupt the voices babbling around me, but before I could say anything, rough hands grabbed hold of my leg, and I looked down into the face of a bearded man.

"Get off that horse, you scum!" yelled the man.

"No," I cried. "I need help for my brother!" I pulled back away from the man.

"You there, Tobias," the man called to a tall, dignified-looking man standing outside the group. "Grab him from the other side!"

"Please, sir," I called to the man called Tobias. "I'm not a thief. Star is helping me. Please get them to listen."

The bearded man's hands reached for my waist. I screamed, and Star reared up again, her front legs flailing. She let out a terrifying neigh at the same time that a bolt of lightning flashed. My jacket whipped open in the wind, and the light from the lightning reflected off the jewels of the horse brooch.

The bearded man crouched back, but Tobias stepped forward and held up a hand. He spoke to Star. "Calm, my beauty. It's all right." She stood still but eyed him warily as he turned to me. "Tell me, please."

My words poured out in a rush. "We, that's my brother Lem and me, have been tryin' to meet Davy Shaw for three days. We walked here from town today, but the rain came, and Lem got really sick. He passed out, and I came for help. He's back at Star's stable. I didn't steal this horse, I swear. I just borrowed her."

A voice sharp as glass cut through the night. "Tobias, bring that child to me. Mr. Reed, take the horse back to her stable and retrieve the sick boy lying there. Bring him to the house, quickly. Margaret, send for Dr. McLean immediately."

I looked toward the voice. The tall figure of a woman stood silhouetted by the light pouring from the open door behind her. I couldn't see her face, but I could see that she was slim, with gray hair piled high on her head, and that she was leaning slightly on a cane.

The people around me immediately reacted to do the woman's bidding.

Tobias patted me on the leg. "There now, child. The missus will take care of everythin'. Mr. Reed," he nodded toward the bearded man, who seemed to be issuing orders of his own to two other men, "he's farm boss here, but he takes his orders from Missus Rutledge. He'll get your brother here right quick." He lifted his arms up toward me.

I smiled at his kind face in relief. I felt suddenly that I had found a friend. I swung a leg over Star's back and slid down into Tobias's arms. As he placed me firmly on the ground, he whispered in my ear, "Now don't let the missus scare you none. She can seem harsh at times, but she's a good lady, all the same."

I nodded and turned to Star. She lowered her head to look me in the eyes, like she had in the stable. I threw my arms around her neck. "Oh, Star, you sweetheart of a horse! Thank you so much for helping us."

Mr. Reed returned and gave me a funny look as I stepped back so he could put a bridle on Star. She submitted to the bridle with no trouble and meekly followed him as he led her to a waiting horse van.

I squared my shoulders and followed Tobias. Miz Rutledge had disappeared but was supposedly waiting for me somewhere in that big house. We climbed the steps and entered through the open front door. I got quick glimpses of high-ceilinged rooms filled with furniture. Tobias's measured steps soon led me to a small, book-lined study dominated by a massive desk. Miz Rutledge sat, silent and watchful, behind the desk. She nodded to a chair, and I gingerly sat down, aware of the damage my wet clothes might do to the yellow damask seat cushion.

Miz Rutledge did not seem concerned about the chair. She gazed at me with disconcerting and somehow familiar blue eyes over her steepled fingers. She nodded at Tobias, and he bowed himself out of the room, closing the door behind him.

The woman continued to stare at me for several long moments without speaking. I took the opportunity to steal glances at the books that lined the walls. Alcott...Austen...Bronte...Dickens. I lost myself in an internal debate about which book I would choose first.

"Where did you get that brooch?" The harsh words brought me back to the present in a heartbeat.

"From m...m...my mother, m...ma'am," I said, sounding like the boy in the jewelry store. I remembered Tobias's warning and sat up straighter, looking my interrogator in the eye. "Lillian Soames is my mother. Calton Soames is my father. Did you know him? He used to train horses."

"Did I know him?" she asked incredulously. She pounded a fist on the desk. "Calton Soames ruined my life. He took precious things from this house and brought death to my family!"

She pointed a finger over my head. I turned around and gazed in shock at a large portrait of a distinguished man with dark hair slicked back over a wide forehead. He stood with one hand resting on a stack of books. Kind, dark eyes looked into mine over a wide, laughing grin. I knew immediately whose portrait this was.

Chapter Twelve

I couldn't accept what I had just heard. I knew Pap had secrets, but my
heart told me that he could not kill any man, especially a man who had
owned this great farm, in cold blood.

I jumped to my feet, thunderstruck. "Why do you say that? I don't
believe it!" I headed to the door, but she stopped me with a word.

"Wait, girl!"

I spun around. "So you know I'm Calton Soames's daughter, not his
son. Makes no difference; I still won't stay and hear him called a
murderer."

To my amazement, Miz Rutledge laughed. "Oh yes, you are your
father's daughter, I see. And take off that ridiculous cap!" I did as she
demanded, shaking out my wet curls. "No, Calton did not murder my
husband, but his actions led to my J.L.'s death all the same. So I do not
know that I owe any kindness to Calton's children."

I debated how to respond. Lem would be brought here any minute, but I knew he was in no shape to move on. And where would we go with no money and no friends?

Miz Rutledge spoke again. "However, I was…fond of your mother." She stared off in space for a moment and then barked, "Tell me about the rest of your family."

I edged back to the chair. "My brother Lemuel David just turned sixteen. I'm thirteen and a half. My brother Calton Jr. who we call C.J. is two, and my baby sister Emmaline Louise is a year old."

"Lemuel…Emmaline," she murmured, closing her blue eyes briefly.

"Yes," I said, uncertainly.

My interrogator was back. "And where do you live?" I told her about Whitburn and why we had run away.

Miz Rutledge leaned back in her chair and drummed her fingers on the desk. "So you came looking for Davy, hoping for jobs, hmm? Well, Davy won't be back until tomorrow." She leaned over the desk and pointed at me. "What made you try to ride that horse, girl? I wouldn't think a coal miner's daughter would have much experience riding race horses." Her lips curled at me mockingly.

I drew myself up tall in the chair. "I've never been on a horse before, ma'am. But Lem was unconscious, and I had to do somethin'. Besides, Star was easy to ride."

"Star?"

"Oh," I said, embarrassed. "I just called her that since she has a white star on her forehead."

"What's your name?" Miz Rutledge asked suddenly.

"Why, it's Destiny Rose, but everybody calls me Dessie."

"Well, Destiny Rose, by quite a coincidence, the name of that horse is Star of Destiny, and not one jockey in Lexington has been able to stay on her. Somehow, you have formed a bond with a horse that shares your name. Rutledge Farms needs Star of Destiny trained for the Derby, which means that, for now, Rutledge Farms needs you!"

Again, I was amazed. We stared at each other over the massive desk, both at a loss for words. A commotion outside the room caught our attention. Tobias knocked and stuck his head in the doorway.

"The young man has been put in the first guest bedroom, missus. Dr. McLean just arrived and has gone up to him."

"Thank you, Tobias. We will come." Miz Rutledge stood and motioned for me to do the same. I was already halfway out of the room, anxious to see Lem. I stood back just inside the door, however, unsure of how to get to Lem's bedroom.

Miz Rutledge nodded and swept before me. She led the way to a grand staircase and up to the second floor. I rushed into the room she indicated.

A white-haired man leaned over the bed, listening through a stethoscope to Lem's chest. I stood at the foot of the bed and waited, my hands twisting the damp hem of my jacket. Miz Rutledge regally took a seat in a nearby chair and placed her hands on the head of her cane, waiting for the doctor to give his report.

Lem did not seem to have regained consciousness. His skin was so pale, and his breathing was labored. He stirred and mumbled my name. I started forward, but the old lady tapped her cane and I stilled.

After several long moments, the doctor stood and addressed Miz Rutledge. "Well, Emily, the boy has caught the influenza, but his lungs appear clear, so I do not think it has become pneumonia. What he needs now is rest and plenty of fluids."

"Thank you, Howard. I do appreciate you coming this late."

I couldn't wait any longer. "Can I talk to him, doctor? He's my brother."

The man turned and looked at me kindly through wire spectacles. "Yes, of course. But don't expect him to talk to you just yet, my dear. He is no longer unconscious, but he is sleeping, which is best. He should come round tomorrow, but he needs to stay in bed for now."

I rushed to Lem's side and took one of his hands. It was as cold as ice, so I rubbed it in both my hands to warm him. I was barely aware of the doctor and the mistress of the house leaving the room and murmuring in the hallway. A few minutes later, Tobias and the servant Miz Rutledge had called Margaret came in.

Tobias tapped me gently on the shoulder. "Miss Dessie? Missus says to let Margaret sit with him a while."

"No, I want to stay with Lem."

"You need to look after yourself first."

I didn't understand what he meant and looked at him curiously.

Tobias shook his head sorrowfully. "I am so sorry, Miss Dessie, but you smell like a goat!"

The truth of his words sank in, and I looked down at myself. My drying clothes hung on me in stiff, awkward angles. I took a sniff and realized that the past three days of hard living and no bathing had taken their toll.

My stomach growled loudly, surprising us both.

Tobias's grin lit up his normally somber features. "Missus told Camille to get some food for you, too. But first, a bath."

I glanced down at Lem and saw he was now sleeping peacefully. I nodded at Margaret, who had settled into a nearby chair with a lapful of knitting.

Tobias led me down the hall and opened the door to the room next to Lem's. It was a beautiful room. The canopied bed was covered in a lacy white coverlet, and next to the two floor-to-ceiling windows, pink roses frolicked across the curtains. Tobias went to a door in one of the walls and opened it to reveal a luxurious bathroom. Creamy white marble covered the floor and counters. A huge claw-footed bathtub stood in the center of the room, full of bubbles. Tobias carefully laid out a thick pink towel and matching washcloth.

"Miss Dessie, you will find dry clothes on the bed. I will return to take your clothes to the laundry. Is there anything else you need?"

I could hardly wait to get in that tub. "Oh, no, Tobias. This is wonderful. Thank you."

Tobias smiled again and bowed out. I took off my jacket and carefully unpinned the brooch and set it down next to the gleaming sink. Then I shed the rest of my filthy clothes and sank gratefully into the warm water. As I lay back, I recalled my daydream of a jolly grandfather who would dump me into a bubble bath with my clothes on. This wasn't quite the way I had dreamed it, but life had definitely taken a turn for the better.

My stomach rumbled again, and I hurried to scrub myself clean so I could go find out what Camille was fixing for me to eat.

***

I awoke the next day hardly daring to believe my surroundings. I stretched and looked out the window to see a sunny day. By the position of the sun, I realized I had slept away most of the morning. I scrambled into a cotton dress and sweater and ran my hands quickly through my hair.

I hurried down the hall to Lem's bedroom and pushed open the door. He was sitting up eating a bowl of oatmeal. Lem smiled weakly when he saw me and put the bowl aside.

"Lem, you're awake. I'm so glad you're better." I rushed to his bedside and felt his forehead. "Yep, your fever's gone."

"Dess, where are we?"

"We're in the big house at Rutledge Farms. Scoot over and I'll tell you what happened yesterday while you were out cold." I climbed in next to him and started to rub his temples. Lem let out a contented sigh as I told the story. I skipped over Miz Rutledge's charge that Pap had caused her husband's death. I needed to learn more first.

True to form, he only interrupted to ask questions about Star.

"So Miz Rutledge thinks you can help train Star of Destiny for the Derby? But you don't know the first thing about horses!"

"I know, but you do. So you'll help me, right? Together, we'll do whatever that old biddy wants so we can stay here. Besides, Star is one sweet horse."

"You shouldn't call Miz Rutledge names," Lem scolded, trying to look stern but not quite achieving it.

"You didn't see her firin' questions and pointin' her finger at me. She was like Old Miz Newly back home. Remember how she made me draw a circle on the blackboard in fourth grade and stand with my nose in the middle of it when I would talk back?"

Lem laughed. "You stopped talkin' back after about a hundred times of standin' at the board though." Lem's laughter turned into coughing. I pounded him on the back.

"Oh Lem, I'm sorry. I didn't mean to make you worse."

"Its' okay, Dess," Lem said as his coughs subsided. "It feels good to laugh. I can't wait to meet Miz Rutledge and see for myself if she's like Miz Newly."

"You can meet me right now, young man," came that clear, sharp voice from the doorway. "And you, young miss, get out of that bed this instant!"

I jumped and jostled Lem's poor head. He sank back on his pillow, and I backed away. Miz Rutledge leaned over and repeated my action of feeling his forehead. She nodded in satisfaction.

"Ah, good. The fever has broken." She spied the half-eaten bowl of oatmeal on the bedside table. She looked at Lem, and her face softened. "I know you may not have much of an appetite, Lemuel, but you need to eat to recover."

"Yes'm," Lem mumbled.

Miz Rutledge settled herself in the chair next to the bed while I stood awkwardly by the window. "Now that Lemuel is getting better, I will tell you what I have decided to do about you both. Davy has returned this morning. After lunch, I will introduce him to Destiny. I have directed Tobias to have two cots placed in the tack room next to Davy's room in the building across from the bunkhouse, and when Lemuel is well, the two of you will move there." She paused and looked sternly at me. "I trust these arrangements are satisfactory."

"Yes, of course, Miz Rutledge. That sounds fine. Thank you kindly." Inside my head I was mourning the loss of the canopy bed and claw-footed tub, but of course we couldn't stay in the mansion. We weren't family, and we were lucky to be allowed to stay at all.

The old lady nodded. "I assume your sister has told you about her extraordinary ride of yesterday evening, Lemuel. It was extraordinary because Star of Destiny has not allowed any jockey to ride her since she came to Rutledge Farms, yet she did your sister's bidding on short acquaintance. Star is one of two Rutledge entries to the Derby this year. You two will work with Davy to train her as quickly as possible."

"Yes, ma'am, we will," I said enthusiastically.

She glared at me again. "I was not asking a question. Either you work with Davy, which is what you came here to do, or you are out the door."

I looked at my feet and felt my face flush with a combination of embarrassment and fury. To calm myself, I balled my fists into the pockets of my dress and rubbed a thumb over the horse brooch pinned to an inside pocket.

She stood and looked down at Lem, her face softening again. She actually reached down and smoothed a lock of his blond hair back from his face. "You remind me so much of your mother," she said softly. I realized why Miz Rutledge had taken a dislike to me. I reminded her of Pap, with my brown curly hair and my outspoken ways. I sighed, thinking that at least she liked Lem, like all adults.

Miz Rutledge looked at me sharply. As though to make up for her moment of weakness, she barked out, "Destiny, you've gotten that dress all wrinkled from climbing in and out of Lemuel's bed. Go dampen it and smooth out the wrinkles. I want you to be presentable when you meet Davy. You may eat your lunch here with Lemuel at noon if you promise me you will not climb into this bed again."

"Yes'm. I mean, yes, ma'am."

"One more thing. You will both be tutored, by me, three days a week for an hour each. I will not have you neglecting your studies. I assume that you are both good students."

Lem and I could only nod silently and hope to live up to her expectations.

"Good morning." Miz Rutledge started to leave the room.

"Miz Rutledge?" She paused at the door to hear my request. "Could I have a piece of paper and an envelope, please? I want to write a letter to Mam and let her know we're all right. I guess she's powerful worried by now."

I waited as she pondered. I was learning that the mistress of the house considered choices carefully but acted forcefully.

"Yes, of course. I think writing home is a very good idea. I will have Margaret bring writing materials. Give your letter to Tobias to post when it's ready."

"Thank you, ma'am," we chorused together to her retreating figure.

She stopped to look back over her shoulder. "And be sure to ask your mother to give my regards to Old Miz Newly," she said and swept from the room.

Lem and I looked at each other in amazement and then broke into giggles. Miz Rutledge had actually made a joke! It seemed that every cloud did have a silver lining. I sobered quickly. It also meant that she had heard what I had said about her. I sighed again. I guessed that in my life, every silver lining had a cloud.

When Margaret brought us paper, pen and an envelope, I composed the letter to Mam with Lem's help:

March 13, 1933

Dear Mam,

We are fine. Lem has been sick, but he's getting better. We are in Lexington and will be working at Rutledge Farms. Miz Rutledge has put us up for a couple of days, but soon we'll be living in the tack room near Davy Shaw. We are really sorry that we ran off and worried you, but I made Lem come with me because I couldn't let him work in the mine any longer. If we ever make any money, we will send some to you for C.J. and Emmie.

We miss you and love you,

Dessie and Lem

Lunch was soup for Lem and a roast beef sandwich for me. Soon it was time for me to head downstairs to see Miz Rutledge and finally meet Davy Shaw. I left Lem behind to take a nap with a promise to tell him all about Davy later.

I retraced my steps of the night before to Miz Rutledge's study. I knocked on the door, but she did not respond. I stood there awkwardly for a moment, unsure what to do, when the door was suddenly yanked open and I was face-to-face with an elf. At least, that's what the creature looked like to me.

The man was my exact height, so I was looking straight into smiling, bright green eyes. White hair covered his head and circled his mouth and chin. He was wearing scarlet suspenders over his blue work shirt and dungarees, and he held a pipe in the hand that was not clasping the doorknob.

"Glory be, you must be Dessie Soames. Come in here, gal, and let me get a good look at you." The elf beckoned me into the room, so I obliged. Miz Rutledge was nowhere to be seen.

"You do have the look of our Cal, don't you? Same brown eyes and curly hair. And if I don't mistake it, you have the same love of mischief, aye?"

"Well, not exactly, sir," I mumbled, not sure what to say.

"Ah, Dessie gal, I'm just kiddin' you." He grinned and stuck out a hand. "The name's Davy Shaw, of course. I understand you and your brother came lookin' for me. Well, here I be." I shook his hand uncertainly, and Davy burst into a fit of laughter. I wasn't sure what was so hilarious, but I was sure that I liked this funny little man already.

He stopped laughing and ushered me to the sofa at one side of the room. He plopped down next to me.

"Now tell me, how is your father? I haven't seen him in many a year, but we were fine friends once, you know." To my surprise, Davy Shaw looked heartbroken at these words, pulled out a handkerchief from his pocket and loudly blew his nose.

"Pap is well, sir. He's a coal miner in Whitburn. Mam is with him, along with our little brother and sister."

"Four children; imagine that. And Lillian is well too?" I nodded, and he turned a stern look on me. "Now one thing we have to get straight right away, Dessie."

"Yes?"

He broke into a grin again. "None of this *sir* business. I want you and your brother to call me Davy. Got it?"

"Yes…Davy," I said, matching his smile.

He bit on his pipe and rubbed his hands together. "All right now. Down to business."

"Excuse me, but shouldn't we wait for Miz Rutledge?"

"Oh, Emily will be along when the mood strikes her, but we don't have to wait on her." I stared at Davy in amazement. Even if I hadn't been drawn to him before, I would have sworn undying devotion now to this man who apparently wasn't intimidated at all by the mistress of Rutledge Farms. "Now, let me explain a couple of things to you. I am the stable manager at Rutledge, which means that Arthur Reed, who runs the farm, and Silas Dimkins, who is the head trainer, well, they take orders from me. You and your brother will work with me, and I will supervise you directly, which isn't the usual way for stable hands. But I don't think Silas will be complainin'. Fact is, Dessie, you've already made an enemy out of him, though I don't think that was your fault, now, was it?" He winked again, and a vision of Star kicking Silas Dimkins flashed through my mind.

Davy continued. "I've been sayin' for months that our Star has a mind of her own and we just have to find what appeals to her. And now Emily tells me that the answer is a spit of a gal!" He indicated me with a sweeping gesture of his hands.

"I sure hope so, Davy. Star let me ride her all right, but it was an emergency. I don't know what she'll do in the daytime."

"We'll find out tomorrow when the boys move Star over to the main stable. In the meantime, I want you to keep away from Mr. Dimkins until you and Lem are settled in with me and Star. It's really Silas's job to train the Rutledge horses, but he's hoppin' mad right now. First thing he said to me when I got back was that he wouldn't work with the fool gal or that blasted horse. He's got his hands full with trainin' Prince of Egypt, Rutledge's other Derby horse, anyway."

I promised to do my best to avoid Silas Dimkins. That suited me fine, and I didn't want to cause further trouble for Davy or for Miz Rutledge.

"Now, little gal, I see that Emily's got you dolled up in a dress today, but you'll need to wear dungarees or overalls when you're in the stable." I nodded happily. I could no longer pass for a boy, since my secret was out, but apparently I could still dress like one. "You and Lem will work long hours, as long as Star can handle. It won't be easy work, but if we can get that horse to do what I think is in her, she may have a shot at the Derby."

"What nonsense are you telling this child, Davy?" demanded Miz Rutledge as she walked into the room. "Prince of Egypt is Rutledge's best Derby hope. I don't know why I let you talk me into keeping Star's name in once we realized we'd been sold a crazy horse. I will be content if you can just get her sufficiently ready to run in the race and not embarrass us."

"All right, Emily, but don't give up hope yet. I'm quite taken with this little gal already. Maybe a guardian angel has sent Dessie and her brother to us."

"Oh, don't be ridiculous. Where was your guardian angel when Billy Tucker broke his collarbone and we had to search for a new jockey? Or when water seeped into the grain bin, ruining three months' of oats?" Miz Rutledge's mouth was set in a straight, firm line.

"We've had a run of bad luck, that's for sure. So we're due some good luck, and these young ones may be what we need." Davy grinned, and after a few moments, Miz Rutledge's mouth quirked into a fleeting smile.

I tried and failed to suppress a giggle.

Miz Rutledge turned brisk. "Dessie should go check on her brother now, Davy. You have monopolized her time long enough." She waved a hand at the bookshelves lining the walls. "Why don't you choose a book to read aloud to Lemuel? He might like that."

All the questions I wanted to ask died on my lips. I looked at Davy, and he sent me a sly wink, so I figured I might be able to get more information another time. For now, I eagerly hurried to look over the book titles before me. In moments, I had found the perfect book for Lem.

It was about a horse and was called *Black Beauty*.

Chapter Thirteen

The next morning, I joined Davy in the smaller of the two buildings in the stable yard. This building, called Stable Hall, held a large indoor paddock, a row of stable stalls, Davy's bedroom and office, and the tack room. The offices for Mr. Dimkins and Mr. Reed were located in the other building across the yard, along with the bunkhouse for the stable hands, a kitchen, and a large room where the workers ate and lounged.

I learned this from Davy. He gave me a quick tour of Stable Hall and then proudly showed me the changes he had made to the tack room to convert part of it to a bedroom for Lem and me. Two cots lined the walls next to a short dresser and lamp. Davy had even scrounged up a colorful rug for the floor.

Impulsively, I thanked him with a hug. He pushed me away quickly, but his grin said he was pleased. Davy told me that the bunkhouse was off limits for us and that we'd eat with him in his office.

In the paddock, a horse was snorting angrily and running frantically in circles. I squealed happily, and Star of Destiny turned and trotted to me. I held my hand over the fence, and she lowered her head, letting me scratch her nose.

"Ooh-ee, if I hadn't seen it with my own eyes, I wouldn't have believed it," said Davy, delighted. "That horse is wild with everybody else but came to you like a trained pup."

I smiled and looked into Star's beautiful, liquid brown eyes. "You're a beauty, my good, good girl. Thank you for helping me," I told her. "Lem is getting better and will be able to meet you soon."

I pulled out the apple Camille had given me and held it toward Star. She took the apple from my hand and munched contentedly.

"Here, gal, why don't you brush her down?" Davy gave me a brush, and I climbed over the fence. He handed me a stool to stand on so I could reach her neck and mane. I had never brushed a horse before, so Davy gave me directions until I had the hang of it. Star stood still while I brushed, occasionally looking back at me as though to check my handiwork.

"You've got it now," said Davy as he settled against the fence and tamped tobacco down in his pipe.

"Davy, why doesn't Miz Rutledge think Star can win the Derby?"

"Well, you heard Emily and me arguin' a bit last night. Rutledge Farms has had a horse in the Derby every year since 1917, but we've never won. Emily decided we'd have two entries this year to up our odds. She bought Star of Destiny from a farm in New York. Star had won every race as a two-year-old, and there was even talk in racin' circles that she'd win the Derby. Then suddenly her owner put her up for sale." Davy took a deep puff of his pipe.

"And…"

Davy removed the pipe from his mouth. "And…Emily bought her without askin' too many questions. When the trailer brought her to Kentucky, we found out why the old coot sold her. The horse was spooked. She's kicked holes in all the stalls she's been in, which is why she was stabled by herself. Worse, though, is that no one's been able to stay on her back more than a few seconds—until you, that is."

"Somethin' happened to her, didn't it? To make her wild, I mean."

"You reckoned that out right quick. Turns out there'd been a stable fire at Heartland Farms, and most of the other horses in the stable died. Star survived, of course, but she wasn't the same."

"Lem and me, we were in a fire too, not long ago."

Davy took a long drag on his pipe before he spoke again. "Dessie gal, could be you and this horse are kindred spirits. That might explain the connection you have. But Star likin' you won't be enough. The fact is that in the Derby, she has to be able to handle a rider and run in a field of horses. And the second fact is that Rutledge Farms needs purse money and the trainin' and breedin' business that comes with a Derby winner."

"Do you mean that Miz Rutledge is broke?"

Davy puffed a series of smoke rings. "Let's just say that we've had a couple of losin' seasons and we can't afford another. The farm's had a run of bad luck. We had two foals that were stillborn, and like Emily said, we've had jockey troubles. Fred Newsom is our newest. You'll meet him when I think he's ready for another try on Star. He lasted all of four seconds last time." Davy chuckled.

"Is there anyone who might try to hurt Rutledge Farms or Miz Rutledge?" I asked, wanting him to stay on that intriguing topic. "Tough as she is, I still would hate to think of her losin' the farm."

He peered at me intently through a haze of smoke. "Little gal, I've pondered on that question long hours and come up empty. I reckon all you and me can do is get Star ready to race and keep our eyes and ears open in the meantime."

Star snorted and nodded, seemingly in agreement. Davy and I laughed, and I patted the now smooth and gleaming coat.

"Time to get our girl geared up for ridin'." Davy nodded to a bridle and saddle hanging on the top rail of the paddock fence.

I gulped back a protest, laid the brush aside and retrieved the gear.

"We'll take it nice and slow for Star," Davy said, but I had the feeling he knew I was the one who was the most nervous. Davy talked me through the first steps of saddling a horse since I'd never done that before either. Star stood quietly and allowed me to insert the bit between her teeth with only a few words of coaxing. Once it was in her mouth, she started to get agitated, so I patted her and whispered to her until she was calm. Davy watched and nodded as though we had all the time in the world.

Lem's words came back to me from the first time we'd seen Star. I turned away from the saddle, climbed the fence and called her over.

"What are you doin'?"

"Lem says to ride a horse bareback first. Besides, that's how she let me on the other night. So I think I should try it this way, okay?"

Davy grinned around the stem of the pipe in his mouth. "Okay by me if it's okay by Star."

I gazed into the horse's dark eyes. "Here, my beauty. I'll just be on your back for a little while, if that's all right with you." She stood still, and I slipped onto her back. I reached for the reins and straightened, trying to quiet the wild drumbeat of my heart.

Davy spoke softly. "Well done, Dessie. Now try to get her to walk slowly around the paddock."

I didn't want to kick her in the sides, even without spurs, so I made a clicking sound with my teeth instead. Star lifted her head and walked slowly around the paddock in a wide circle. I looked over at Davy, who gave me a grin and a thumbs-up. I understood a tiny bit why Lem loved riding horses so much. On Star's back, I felt like I could do or be anything. I couldn't stop smiling. Star turned her head and looked back at me, and I knew we were connected in some deep, primal way.

Davy called out instructions as I practiced using the reins and my knees to guide Star through turns. We did about twenty circuits around the paddock, and then he called us over for a break. I climbed down, rubbing my sore backside while Davy held out a handful of oats to Star.

"Ready to try her with a saddle?"

"Yes, I think so, but you'll have to show me how to put it on."

Davy nodded. "Talk to Star as I do this, but watch me so you can do it the next time."

I stood at the side of Star's head, patting her and whispering encouragement, my gaze fixed on Davy's every move.

"And the last step is to wait a moment and see if the cinch needs tightenin'. Some horses learn the trick of puffing out their chests so the cinch is loose when they go to breathe regular. Looks like Star isn't tryin' that one on us though." He patted her side and turned to me, his hands cupped.

I hesitated a second and then realized what I was expected to do. I placed my left foot in Davy's hands, and he lifted me up while I swung my right leg over and then settled my feet in the stirrups.

I immediately felt Star stiffen under me, so I sat as still as I could and just whispered to her for several minutes. I didn't try to get her to move until I knew she was calm again. Davy puffed on his pipe and waited patiently.

I made the clicking sound again, and Star began another slow circuit around the paddock. Once she was comfortable walking with me in the saddle, Davy taught me to get Star to trot. At first I was terrified but reminded myself that Star wouldn't let me fall. I relaxed my tensed shoulders back, and beneath me, I could feel Star relax too. As the horse gained speed, we melded together into a perfect rhythm, and I let out a whoop of joy.

Davy beamed and nodded his approval as we trotted around and around the enclosure. Before I was ready, he gestured for me to slow Star down to a walk. I did so reluctantly, and we joined him at the gate.

"Davy, that was so great! I don't know what I was scared of." I patted Star's neck. "Oh, you wonderful girl." Star snorted softly in agreement.

"Just look at you riding that horse!" called a familiar voice.

I looked up to see Lem walking slowly through the door with the help of a tall, bearded man. The man had hold of Lem's arm with one hand, and in his other hand, he held a bulging knapsack.

"Lem! I thought you weren't coming over until tomorrow." I swung out of the saddle and hurried to meet my brother.

"This young man has been driving Tobias and Miz Rutledge batty all morning. It seems he just couldn't let his sister have all the fun." Mr. Reed's hearty voice boomed through the paddock. I was so surprised by his change in attitude from the night I rode Star to the manor house that I just stared at him. Lem came to my rescue.

"I'm feeling much better now, Dess. The doc says I have to take it easy for a couple more days, but Miz Emily gave me the go-ahead to move in over here. Mr. Reed volunteered to help bring my bits and pieces. Thank you, sir."

"Glad to be of service, my boy," stated Mr. Reed as he led Lem to a nearby bale of hay. "You rest a while." He turned to me. "Dessie, I want to make amends for my actions the other night. Obviously, I was mistaken when I took you to be a horse thief. I hope we can be friends."

I hesitated, remembering the rough way Mr. Reed had tried to pull me off the horse. He kept smiling, his teeth hidden behind a bushy mustache, waiting for me to respond. "Uhm, sure," I said, reluctantly.

If Mr. Reed noticed that my response was halfhearted, he didn't show it. "That's better. Now, Davy, I need a bit of your time."

"Certainly, Arthur. Let's go to my office." Davy winked at us as he passed.

As soon as the men were out of sight, I hissed at Lem. "Since when did you and that man become such pals?"

"Yesterday evening, actually. He came to visit me after you said goodnight. He brought me some horse racing magazines. I think he's all right."

"Oh, I guess; if you say so." I shrugged my shoulders and dismissed all thoughts of Mr. Reed. "Davy's swell, though, isn't he? He's been so patient with me and Star today."

"You were really ridin', Dess! It was a sight to behold. Mam would be so proud. You know how she loves horses."

I pushed all thoughts of Mam and our family away, and instead, I told my brother what Davy had shared with me about Star being in a fire.

"So, I did what you said. I rode her bareback at first until she was calm, and then Davy showed me how to saddle her. I really like riding Star, Lem, but I can't wait to see you ride her. She'll make you fly, I bet."

"I can't wait either. Dess, you really did it, you know. You said you'd get us new lives on a horse farm. I guess you can do just about anything."

I looked at my feet, embarrassed. "I think luck and maybe a guardian angel or two helped us out."

Lem started to protest but was interrupted by a loud "so long" from Mr. Reed, followed by Davy's return. The elf-man's eyes twinkled as he relit his pipe.

"Hello there, Lem. I'm right pleased to meet you. I guess Dessie has been bringin' you up to speed? Good, good. Now, let me tell you both what I'm thinkin'. It's clear that Dessie and Star have a strong bond, so I'd like to train Dessie to pony Star at the Derby."

Lem gasped. "Oh, that'd be a gas!"

"Me ride in the Derby? I couldn't!"

Davy and Lem laughed, and I fumed at them. "I don't see what's so funny. I'm not the one who wants to be a jockey, you know."

"To pony a racehorse just means to ride another horse next to the racehorse and jockey on their way to get in position on the track," said Lem. "It's a huge honor to get to do that."

"Since Star trusts you so, Dessie, she'd be most at ease having you with her up to that point."

"Oh. I guess I could do that. But what about Lem? He's the real horse expert, not me."

Davy blew out a smoke ring and looked intently at Lem. "If you are half the rider your sister believes you to be, I'll make you an apprentice jockey, and you can ride Star during her practice runs when Fred's away. How about it, son?"

Lem's eyes shone as he held out a hand and solemnly shook the one Davy offered. "I won't let you down. I promise."

"Alrighty then. Let's stow Lem's gear, and I'll get us some grub."

The little man tossed Lem's knapsack over his shoulder and skipped toward our room. I put an arm around Lem's waist, and we followed slowly, both grinning like fools.

***

Lem was as charmed by our quarters as I was. We had slept in one room our whole lives, so it felt unnatural to be apart in separate rooms in the big house. Plus, I had been holding my breath and tiptoeing whenever I passed a room where Miz Emily might be. Living in Stable Hall with Davy on the other side of the wall and Star settled in a big, comfortable stall on the other side of the paddock seemed pretty close to heaven.

The next few weeks became a dizzying round of practice drills, riding lessons, tutoring from Miz Emily in grammar and ciphering and, my least favorite task, mucking out stalls. Although there were some days when I would gladly have traded a shovel of horse manure for the agony of sitting under Miz Emily's stony gaze as I tried to conjugate verbs or perform long division.

Seven days a week, Davy woke us for an early morning practice session on the half-mile track down a lane at the rear of the manor house. As promised, Lem was Star's rider during these practices. Star had accepted Lem on her back in the Stable Hall paddock as easily as she had me. I guessed she could sense how close he and I were.

I'll never forget the first time Lem took Star out on the track. The sun had just peeked over the horizon as we walked down the lane in companionable silence. The dew glistened on the grass and on the tips of the crocuses just pushing up through the earth. Davy and I stood by the fence, stamping our feet now and then to keep warm.

Lem led Star onto the track and swung up into the saddle. He leaned low over Star's neck, whispered in her ear and they were off, into a full gallop in the blink of an eye. They practically flew around that track. The boy and the horse seemed to have been born for each other, so perfectly were they matched. My eyes got misty, and the word destiny came to mind. It might be my name, but I knew right then I was watching Lem find his true and rightful purpose.

I looked at Davy and realized he was feeling the same. He pulled out his handkerchief and noisily blew his nose. The spell was broken, and we leaned together, dissolving into giggles.

Davy waved Lem and Star over, and when they reached us, he launched into a litany of directions to improve Lem's technique. I scratched Star between the eyes and slipped her some sugar cubes I'd swiped from yesterday's dinner.

My mind drifted while the menfolk droned on until my attention was caught by another group entering the practice track at the opposite side from us. Silas Dimkins barked orders to a thin man sitting on an enormous gray stallion. I realized this must be Prince of Egypt, the other Rutledge Derby entry. His bearing was truly regal, and he showed the classic signs of a Thoroughbred that Davy had taught me. The gray's well-chiseled head sat atop a long neck that sloped down to meet his high-set withers and short back. His chest was deep, his legs long and his body lean.

Comparing Prince to Star, I could understand why Miz Emily felt he had the better chance to win the race. Star stood a good hand and a half shorter than Prince and was smaller and slimmer. Davy had told me that Prince was built to be a sprinter, but Star was the unusual combination of being a distance runner that could also sprint. Or she had done so, before the stable fire.

I turned my attention to the rider and realized with a start that he was the man who had called to Lem and me the first day we'd come to Rutledge and been sent away by Silas Dimkins. Here was the good

Samaritan who had told us that Davy would return in three days. He had shown a dislike for Mr. Dimkins that day and now sat with his head bowed as the trainer lashed him with sharp words. I felt sorry for the nameless fellow. Apparently feeling my gaze on him, he suddenly looked up at me and winked, causing my nemesis to halt in mid-sentence.

"Uh-oh," I said as Mr. Dimkins strode purposely toward us.

Davy looked over from where he was showing Lem a proper rein hold and hurried to stand in front of me. "Hello there, Silas," he boomed. "A fine morning, isn't it?"

"Just what do you think you're playing at, Davy? You know this is Prince's practice time." The trainer sneered in my direction. "Get those children and that nag off my track."

Davy's eyes narrowed as he took a long drag on his ever-present pipe and slowly blew out a stream of smoke. Silas Dimkins shifted uneasily before Davy's steady gaze and lack of response. Davy took the pipe from his mouth and finally spoke.

"Seems to me that you're the one who's a mite confused. This is Miz Emily's track and Miz Emily's workers and Miz Emily's Derby entries. We share this track, Silas. Star will practice first and Prince after her every morning and every afternoon. If you have a problem with that, take it up with our boss lady."

"I may just do that!"

"Fine, fine. We can discuss it with Emily at our next Friday lunch meeting. Or rather, I can discuss it with her, since you aren't invited to those, are you now?"

Mr. Dimkins grunted and stalked away.

"Oh, Silas," called Davy.

"Yeah?"

"Don't ever let me hear you call Star of Destiny a nag again or I promise you as sure as my sainted mother gave me life that you will be on a bread line before the day is through."

I started to snigger but turned my laughter into a fit of coughing as the trainer turned on his heel and yelled to Prince's rider, "Roy, the air is too chilly for Prince. Take him back to the stable and bring him out in an hour when the weather is better."

Lem just smiled sweetly as he turned Star back out to another run.

"You sure put him in his place, Davy!" I gushed.

"Shush, child. I need to time your brother," he said, pulling a stopwatch out of his pocket. "Be a good lass and fetch some oats for Star.

She'll be hungry soon, and you know how she can nag if she's kept waitin'."

He flashed a grin at me, and I shook my head at his pun as I went to grab a bucket.

Chapter Fourteen

Three days later, I was sitting at a table on the porch at the rear of the big house, struggling to repeat phrases in French. Miz Emily had decided that I needed to learn the language to become a proper young lady.

"*Non, non*, Destiny. *Parlez-vous francais* is a question. You must raise your voice at the end."

"Yes, Miz Emily. I mean, *Oui, Madame* Rutledge," I said between gritted teeth.

"You must work on your pronunciation. Honestly, I don't believe you are trying at all to improve. Repeat after me, *Comment allez-vous?* Wait, what is going on down there?" Miz Emily rose and limped to the bank of windows that surrounded the veranda. Without turning, she flung out an arm and snapped her fingers at me. "Destiny, get my cane."

I handed it to her and followed as she went down the back steps and across the flagstone path toward the track. We tried to hurry, but her need to use the cane slowed us down.

"Darned rheumatism," she muttered, surprising me.

Ahead, we could see a crowd of men gathering on the track. At first I could not make out what they were all shouting about. Cutting through the din was a terrible, guttural cry that I'd never heard before and never wanted to hear again. I knew instinctively that someone or something was in great pain.

When we got close to the crowd, Miz Emily raised her voice. "Let me through! You there, Andy and Jeb, make way." She plied her cane to the backs of two men, who immediately doffed their caps for her and moved aside. The rest of the crowd parted for their boss lady.

"Oh, Lord have mercy!" she exclaimed.

I peeked around her and saw the horrific sight of Prince of Egypt splayed out on the track, his two front legs twisted under him in weird angles. Roy lay on the track, too, clutching a shoulder with his other hand and moaning loudly. Prince thrashed wildly about, his eyes bulging and his teeth bared. Red-tinged foam fell from his mouth as he bellowed in agony.

Silas Dimkins stood by the horse, ranting at Roy, while Davy knelt by Prince, rubbing his neck and speaking softly to him. Confusion reigned as the other men milled about, shuffling their feet and giving suggestions that no one followed.

"What have you done, you no-good, useless, son of a jackal?" Flecks of spittle gathered in the corners of Silas's mouth and flew about as he yelled. "Get on your feet and off this farm. And if you ever try to ride a horse again, I swear I will hunt you down and break both your arms and your legs, you worthless piece of…"

"Silence!" Miz Emily's voice, sharp and commanding, cut through Silas's words, and he gaped at her, open-mouthed. The rest of the men immediately quieted. "Now, Jeb, you and Lyle take Roy to the house. Tell Tobias to call Dr. McLean and to make Roy comfortable until the doctor arrives. Silas, have you sent for Ben Wheeler?"

I didn't know who that was, but Mr. Dimkins just shook his head and looked down at his feet, breathing heavily.

"Emily, Ben won't be able to do anything for this horse except put him out of his misery. There's no sense in waiting for the vet to get here to do that."

"You're just saying that, Davy, so your precious crazy horse will be the only Rutledge Derby entry!"

Davy's gentle voice showed no anger. "Silas, any fool can see that both of Prince's front legs are broken. This is an awful thing, but he'll never run again." He stood, put a hand on the taller man's shoulder and looked him in the eyes. "You know what must be done."

Mr. Dimkins stared at Davy for a long moment and nodded. Davy looked over at Miz Emily, who said quietly, "Andy, tell Tobias to fetch Mr. Rutledge's pistol."

I stepped to the center of the group. "No! Miz Emily…Davy…Mr. Dimkins…you can't mean to…" I looked angrily from one adult to another. "Prince is a strong horse. You can't just give up on him! Get that Doc Wheeler here. He'll fix him up; I know he will."

Davy turned sad eyes to me. "Dessie, there's no other way."

"I don't believe you! How can you do this, Davy? I thought you were kind, but I guess I was wrong."

At that moment, Lem ran up to the small crowd staring at Davy and me. "What's happened?" He grasped the situation in an instant. "Oh, not Prince!" He knelt down to stroke the terrified horse. "I'm so sorry, Miz Emily."

She sent him a fleeting smile and said gently, "Take Destiny back to your room please, Lemuel."

He stood. "Let's go, Dess."

I shook my head and put my fists on my hips, determined to stand my ground.

Tobias arrived with a large pistol cradled in the crook of an elbow. Davy started to reach for it, but Silas Dimkins roused himself and pushed in front of Davy, saying gruffly, "He's my horse."

Lem put a hand in the small of my back to propel me forward. "Come with me, Dessie, or so help me God, I'll carry you over my shoulder!"

I was so surprised to hear Lem take charge that I didn't protest again until we were around the corner of the house.

"Lem, don't you know what they're doing? We can't let them shoot Prince!" I pulled away to turn back, but my path was blocked by Arthur Reed.

"I thought you might require some help, son," he said to Lem over my head.

"No, sir, but thanks anyway."

"Certainly, certainly." Mr. Reed looked down at me. "I know this seems harsh to you, Dessie, but these things happen on a horse farm. Try not to be too upset." He hurried off toward the track.

A single pistol shot split the air. I threw myself down on a nearby bench.

"I don't understand, Lem. Why did Davy tell them to do that? People break their legs and get better."

"But horses usually don't, especially Thoroughbred horses. Both of Prince's front legs were broken. He wouldn't have even been able to stand while he was mendin'. Davy was right, and so is Mr. Reed. Besides, you heard Prince. He was hurtin' real bad."

"Yeah, he was." I dashed away hot tears and leaned against Lem's shoulder. "This won't happen to Star, will it?"

"I don't know why Prince fell. We'll just have to take extra good care of Star."

I jumped up, suddenly needing to reassure myself that she was all right. "Let's go check on her!" I ran the rest of the way to Star's stall. Lem found us there a few moments later. We spent the rest of that afternoon with Star while the Rutledge men buried Prince of Egypt in a field down the lane.

***

The next day, Miz Emily sent word for me to come to finish our lesson. I tried to cram as I walked over, so my eyes were on the French grammar book as I neared the porch. I was startled by the slamming of the front door and suddenly came face to face with a very angry Silas Dimkins. He grabbed me roughly by the arm.

"Hey, let me go!" I squirmed, but he held on tighter and brought his face in close to mine.

"There's been nothing but trouble since you brats showed up here. If I find out that you and your brother had anything to do with Prince's death, I will break every bone in your bodies, no matter what Miz Emily has to say."

"I don't know what you're talking about. Wasn't it an accident?"

"Oh you're a right good little actress, ain't you, pretending to be innocent and batting those big eyes at me. But everyone knows what your father was. You're his bad seed. I'll be watching your every move from now on. That's a promise!" He wrenched his arm free and stalked away.

I rubbed my aching arm and took deep breaths to calm my shaking. I had guessed Silas Dimkins had a grudge against Pap, but that didn't make it any easier to hear him call me names. I was also mystified why he'd think we would hurt Prince. I picked up my dropped book and hurried into the house.

I burst in on Miz Emily and Davy in her study.

"Destiny, how many times must I remind you to knock before opening a door?" she asked, exasperated.

"I'm sorry," I said automatically. "But Mr. Dimkins just told me it wasn't an accident that Prince got hurt."

"Silas should not have shared that with you. It is not your concern."

"Emily, beggin' your pardon, but I think Dessie and Lem have a right to know. They will be helpin' protect Star, after all."

"Protect Star? Why?" I demanded.

The mistress considered me over her steepled fingers. "Very well. Davy found evidence that Prince's fall was deliberate."

I gasped. "How?"

Davy held out a small piece of fine wire. "I found this on the ground near an inside post on the practice track. Looks like someone strung this wire from that post across the track to the post just inside the north gate opening. Prince hit the wire, tripped and fell. By the time I looked around the track, the rest of the wire was gone, but whoever it was missed this piece."

"Oh, poor Prince! Who would do such a thing?"

"That, my girl, is what we're tryin' to figure out," Davy stated grimly.

"Rather than guess at suspects, Davy, perhaps we need to look at this from the other way around. Who do you trust completely?"

"Hmm, you of course, Emily, and Tobias and Roy, my nephew Andy and Dessie and Lem."

"Not Silas or Arthur?" Miz Emily asked, surprised.

Davy hesitated as he puffed on his pipe. "Silas seems genuinely upset, but that's what you'd expect him to show. And as for Arthur, I didn't see him around when Prince was hurt, which makes a body wonder where he'd got to."

"He came up to Lem and me when we were headin' back to Stable Hall yesterday," I put in. "But my money's on Silas Dimkins. He's a born crook if I ever saw one." I stuck out my arm. "Look what he did to me."

"Destiny! Did Silas make those bruises?"

"Yes, ma'am. And he threatened to hurt me…and Lem. He accused us of causin' Prince's fall."

Miz Emily frowned mightily. "Perhaps you're right. I'll fire Silas immediately."

Davy blew smoke rings. "I wouldn't be so hasty. If Silas is our man, we need him around to watch. He's got to be takin' orders from someone higher up. That's who we really want to find."

"But he's threatened the child!"

I looked in surprise at Miz Emily. She was actually taking up for me.

"I'll look after Dessie. Nobody will hurt her or Lem. I promise." Davy winked at me, and I knew he'd forgiven me for yesterday's harsh words.

I nodded at him. "What about Star? You said she needs protectin'."

Miz Emily sighed. "Star is now Rutledge's only Derby entry. She will have a guard at all times. Davy, draw up a schedule for the men you named, and yes, include Tobias. I'll find someone else to cover his duties until Derby day. In the meantime, I guess we'll trust no one else."

"Aye. I'll put a pallet in Star's stall and sleep in there too. And no, Dessie, you cannot join me."

My shoulders slumped in disappointment.

"Destiny, sit up straight. A lady's posture is very important. Now please get my French grammar book. I left it in the top drawer of the desk on the porch. We'll finish our lesson here."

I hurried to the porch. I crossed to the desk and tugged open the top drawer. I wasn't paying attention and pulled on it so quickly that the whole drawer came out and fell to the floor, spilling all its contents.

I dropped to my hands and knees and gathered papers and pens, heaving a sigh of relief to find that nothing had broken. I laid the French book aside and reached to put the drawer back but found it turned over. As I went to pick it up, I spied a white rectangle stuck in a wooden slat on the bottom of the drawer. I turned it over and realized it was a photograph.

The picture was of the man I knew was Mr. Rutledge from the portrait in Miz Emily's study. He was bouncing a pretty, blond-haired little girl on his knee. Both the man and the girl were smiling widely. Someone had written *Daddy and his girl* across the bottom. My heart constricted at the sight of a happy father and daughter but then did a series of flip-flops when I realized that the girl looked a lot like Lem when he was younger.

The picture blurred as a possible explanation dawned. Could this have been Mam's house when she was growing up? Had I really brought us to her home and her mother? I hadn't seen any portraits or photographs in the house except ones of Mr. and Miz Rutledge. Besides, Miz Emily hadn't exactly welcomed Lem and me like long-lost grandchildren. Her angry words about Pap came back to me. She said that he'd taken precious things from this house. If she meant the jewelry, she hadn't asked for the horse brooch back. Could she still be steamed about Mam taking some bracelets and necklaces? It didn't make much sense that with all her wealth, Miz Emily wouldn't want to know us because of some jewelry, but who knew with rich people?

I remembered she was waiting for me, and I hastily put the drawer in the desk and grabbed the book. I hesitated a moment and then stuck the photograph in a pocket of my overalls. I hurried back to the study where Miz Emily sat alone, drumming her fingers on the desk and staring at her husband's portrait. I hastily sat down and handed her the book.

When we finished our lesson, she held out an envelope. "This came for you and Lemuel yesterday. It's from your mother."

"A letter from Mam! Oh, thank you, Miz Emily." I placed it carefully in the French book and hugged the book to my chest. I hesitated, waiting to see if now was the moment she would tell me she was my grandmother.

"What are you waiting for, girl? Go on with you. I'm sure you have chores to do."

"Yes, ma'am."

"Oh, and Destiny…"

"Yes?" I said expectantly.

"Practice your French phrases. I want to hear perfect diction at our next lesson."

"Oui, oui, Madame!" I slammed the door behind me, not caring if it made her angry.

***

March 30, 1933

Dear Lem and Dessie,

We were so relieved to hear from you. Your pa and I have been worrying ourselves sick. Pap saw you jump into that train car, but we didn't know where you'd gone from there. What a foolish, foolish thing to do! When I see you next, I won't know whether to hug you or yell at you. I'll probably do a bit of both, I suspect.

At any rate, it sounds as if things have worked out well. We're very glad to know you are with Davy and Miz Rutledge. We know them from our days in Lexington. I don't know how you came to find out about them, but we trust them and know they will do their best for you.

Your pa wants to come bring you home, but I am trying to get him to let you stay, at least through the summer. Besides, he can't really take time off from the mine right now since he's doing double shifts. C.J. and Emmie miss you, too.

We send you all our love,

Mam.

That night, I couldn't sleep. Thoughts of Miz Emily, Mam and Pap, C.J., Emmie and Whitburn kept swirling away in my brain. I checked to see if Lem was awake so we could talk, but he was sleeping soundly.

I got up, wrapped my robe around me and went in search of Davy. He was sitting on his pallet in Star's stall, puffing on his pipe. He looked up in surprise.

"Anything wrong, Dessie?"

"I just can't sleep." I patted Star a moment and sat down on a feed sack. "Are you comfortable here, Davy? Is there anything I can get you?"

"I'm fine, gal. I've slept in worse places."

"Good. That's good."

"There's something on your mind."

"Davy, is Miz Emily our grandmother? Lem's and mine?" I blurted out.

He puffed a few times before answering. "Now why would you ask that, I wonder?"

"I found a photograph of Mr. Rutledge and a little girl. She looks like Mam, or at least she looks like Lem did when he was little. Was Mam their little girl?"

Davy blew smoke as he considered. "I guess it's time for you to know the truth, and I guess I might as well be the one to tell it. Yes, your mother was born Lillian Rutledge. She grew up here and was adored by everyone, includin' me. I guess we spoiled her too much, especially her daddy. When she was eighteen, Calton Soames came to Lexington. He was a brilliant trainer, a risin' star. He was also eight years older than Lil, handsome and reckless. I liked Calton a great deal. I showed him the ropes and introduced him to the local racin' circuit. I was also the first to suspect a romance between Cal and the boss's daughter. I didn't share my suspicions with Mr. John or Miz Emily, though. Many a time since, I've wished I had."

Davy took out his handkerchief and rubbed it over his face. I waited for him to continue.

"Before we knew it, Cal and Lil up and eloped. Oh, the ruckus at the big house the day they came home! Of course, Mr. John and Miz Emily had never pictured a man like Cal as a son-in-law. The upshot was that Cal was fired and the young couple was turned out of the house."

"What did they do then?"

"Your pa has a way of landin' on his feet. Only a day or two later, he was trainin' over at Calloway. Lil found a ground-floor apartment in a house downtown, and they settled down. After a few months, Mr. John started droppin' by to check on things, and then slowly Cal and Lil were invited back to the house. I thought the troubles were over."

"Somethin' bad happened, didn't it? What did Pap do?" I whispered.

"I don't know if you know this or not, but your pa won a lot of awards in his short career. He became a name in the business, and people started throwin' jobs and money at him. Big-shot businessmen and politicians invited him to parties, and he started to drink heavily. Rumors flew around that he was takin' on too many clients and was about to crack under the pressure. Now Lillian had a brother, John Lemuel Jr…"

"What? Mam never said."

Davy nodded and went on with his story. "Johnny was a great favorite, too. He was such a jokester; always laughin'. Johnny was in college at Centre but spent a lot of weekends crashin' on the sofa at his sister's. I guess he liked Cal and Lil's place better than his parents' stuffy old mansion. Anyway, on this day, Johnny was at the Soames' place. Cal was home and Lil was out when a fire started in the apartment."

"Oh no," I gasped, remembering Pap mumbling about another fire when I was rescuing the babies from our burning house in Whitburn.

"Cal survived the fire, obviously, but Johnny didn't. I wasn't there, but the story that went around was that Cal had been drinkin' and fell asleep with a lit cigarette and was too drunk to save Johnny."

"Mam lost her brother. That must have been horrible for her."

"That was only the start, little gal. When Mr. John found out about his son's death and Cal's part in it, he cursed Cal. He told him to get off his land and never return. Lillian started to go with Cal, and her father tried to stop her. They were in a struggle when Mr. John suddenly clutched at his chest and collapsed. His heart gave out."

"Oh, Mam…"

I wasn't sure I wanted to hear the rest, but Davy's soft voice continued. "After the double funeral, Miz Emily gave Lillian a choice. She could stay and help her run Rutledge Farms or she could leave with Cal and never return." Davy looked kindly at me. "You know or can guess the rest, Dessie. Your mother chose your pa. They fell on hard times pretty fast. Calton was branded as a bum, a drunk and, unfairly to my mind, a killer. No Thoroughbred owner would hire him. His career as a trainer was over. I lost track of him; didn't know he'd become a coal miner until you and Lem showed up."

"And Miz Emily?"

"Emily put away everythin' that reminded her of her children: the photographs, the portraits, their bits and pieces. She forbade everyone on the farm to ever speak of Lillian or Johnny, and she carried on as if they'd never been born. Until you rode in that stormy night, that is."

I looked at him, surprised. "What do you mean?"

"I know you find her as hard as nails, Dessie, but it's warmed this old man's heart to see her open up her life a crack here and there to let you and Lem in. She could have sent you away, but she didn't. She could have gotten a tutor for you, but she's teachin' you herself. And today, she was ready to fire Silas for layin' his hand on you. Give her time, child. She's comin' around."

"Can I tell Lem about all this?"

"It's his family history too, ain't it? Besides, that boy's not a blabbermouth." Davy grinned around his pipe.

I stood and stretched. "I'll go back to bed now. Thank you for tellin' me."

"You're welcome. Goodnight."

I patted Star once more to say goodnight to her but turned at the door to the stall. "And Davy?" He looked up again.

"I'm sorry I said yesterday that I didn't believe you. I was wrong about Prince."

"Apology accepted. Get on to bed."

I went, and even with all that Davy had shared about Mam and Pap, I was out almost as soon as my head hit the pillow.

A few days later, Davy introduced us to Fred Newsom, the jockey who would ride Star in the Derby. Like all jockeys, Fred was short and slim, matching Lem in size. Shrewd eyes peered out of a weather-beaten face over a grim mouth.

He greeted us sternly. "I was asked to ride Star because I'm known for being able to handle horses that are a bit wild. I've been racing for nigh on fifteen years, and I've never heard of using kids as nursemaids for a racehorse. If either of you get in the way, I'll banish you from the track. Understand?"

"Yes, sir. We won't get in the way," said Lem.

I looked in confusion at Davy, but he just chuckled. "Wait and see, Fred."

Star whinnied, as though in agreement with Davy, and I smiled to myself.

Davy turned to Lem. "Take her out and show Fred what you and our girl can do."

Lem put Star through several furlong sprints to warm her up. Davy waved them into position to do a timed trial of ten furlongs, which I'd learned was the same distance as the Derby at one and a quarter miles. Davy readied his stopwatch and nodded at Fred, who waved his handkerchief. Lem gently nudged Star's flanks, and they were off, speeding past the fence posts and throwing up a cloud of reddish dust in their wake.

When they reached the ten-furlong post, Davy clicked the stopwatch and passed it over to the jockey, his expression neutral.

"Are you sure this is right?"

"Sure I'm sure."

"But this is a full three seconds off last year's Derby time," said Fred.

"Aye. We've been posting times like this for two weeks."

A grin slowly spread until it lit Fred's entire face. "If the filly can do this with that kid, I should be able to shave at least another five seconds off her time. We actually have a chance!"

Davy beamed back. "Aye, I know."

"What do you mean, actually have a chance?" I demanded as Lem pulled Star to a stop and climbed down.

Fred clapped Lem on the back. "That was fine riding, my boy." He turned to me. "Star of Destiny is a long shot. That means the racing world doesn't consider her likely to win."

"Why not?"

"First off, she's a filly, and there's only been one other filly win before and that was Regret, back in 1915. Second, she hasn't won or even been entered in any other stakes race for months. Third, she's got a reputation as being uncontrollable."

"Star's not uncontrollable. Her rider's just got to know how to handle her," said Lem.

"I guess that's where you come in. Let's take Star back to her stall and talk a bit," said the jockey.

"Yes, sir!"

I started to follow, but Davy laid a hand on my arm and steered me toward two horses tied up outside the practice track. "Meet Graceful Lady, Dessie. She'll be your horse at the Derby." He indicated a small brown mare with huge liquid eyes.

"She's lovely, but is she gentle?" I asked nervously.

"She's the gentlest horse around. Up you go. It's time to train you for your Derby job." I swung into the saddle.

By morning's end, Lady and I were old pals. She proved to be easygoing and patient, as promised. We took her to Stable Hall and introduced her to Star, who ignored Lady all afternoon. When it was time to return Star to her stall, though, she nudged Lady along too, so the brown mare was bedded down in the stall next to the black Thoroughbred, and by the end of the week, they were inseparable. Our Derby team was complete.

Chapter Fifteen

The days leading up to the Derby were busy. Davy and Fred increased
Star's practices and kept Lem and me hopping with chores. Since Tobias
was helping guard Star, he was pressed into service to prepare Fred's
silks, the purple and white shirt and cap he would wear during the race.
Tobias found several tears needing repair and decided that would be a
good task for me.

"Jeepers," I groaned as he handed me the needle. "I thought my sewing
days were over."

Tobias smiled and continued polishing Fred's knee-high boots. I bent
over the silks and, despite stabbing my fingers several times, was able to
sew the tears without bleeding on the shirt. Besides, I forgot my pain
when Fred tried them on and judged them ready.

"Ooh-ee," said Davy. "You and Star will make Rutledge Farms proud,
Fred. I'll go tell Miz Emily Star's trial times for this mornin'. She wants
to share them with the whole farm at the party tonight."

"What party?" I demanded.

"Mr. John used to hold a celebration the night before he and Miz Emily took the team to Louisville. The whole farm gathered to eat and listen to speeches and music. Since his death, there's been no Derby party. This year, Miz Emily decided to bring it back." Davy winked at me, and I knew he was thinking that we might be the reason for Miz Emily's change of heart.

"A party! Oh, what will I wear?"

The group around me laughed. "There's a girl inside that tomboy after all," grinned Lem.

I stuck my tongue out at him and hurried to our room to rummage for something nicer than overalls.

***

As the sun set, all of Rutledge Farms gathered behind the big house— all except Andy Shaw, who was on guard duty with Star. I was enchanted by the scene. Three long rows of tables were laid out, covered with an assortment of tablecloths. Oil lamps lit the tables and hung from tree branches. Two tables set a bit apart were loaded with food. Somehow in the midst of the Depression, Miz Emily and Camille had managed a feast. My mouth watered at the sight of huge ham steaks, a mountain of spare ribs, corn pudding, squash, string beans, spoon bread, and a dozen pies.

Lem waved me to a seat next to him. As I sat down, I saw Jeb pass a bottle across the table. I glanced at Lem, but he was deep in conversation with Fred, so he wasn't aware the men were spiking their drinks. There was talk of repealing Prohibition, but it hadn't happened yet. Even so, I decided to keep my mouth shut.

Miz Emily was seated at the head table with Davy, Arthur Reed and Silas Dimkins, along with invited guests. I recognized Dr. McLean and Josiah Hawthorne from the Breeders' Syndicate, but there was another man and a lady I didn't know. Lem said the man was Dr. Wheeler, the veterinarian, and the lady was Mr. Hawthorne's wife. I was watching the lady dig into her third slice of pie and wondering how she could eat that much when I noticed Mr. Hawthorne staring at me. I remembered that the last time he'd seen me, I'd pretended to be a boy named Denny. I ducked my head and tried to hide.

After dinner, Miz Emily rose and delicately tapped a knife to her glass.

"Good evening, everyone. I am pleased that we are able to resume our Derby party tradition. This year, we have much to celebrate. Although saddened to lose our gallant Prince of Egypt," she nodded to Silas,

"Davy tells me Star of Destiny has trained well with Fred and we have a good chance at winning. Her practice time today beat last year's winner by 3.2 seconds."

The crowd cheered, and Miz Emily waited for quiet. "As you know, Star was wild when she came to Rutledge, but with the help of Davy and two young friends, she is ready to race again." The crowd cheered again, calling our names. Jeb slapped me on the back so hard I almost landed facedown in chocolate pie.

Miz Emily continued. "So tomorrow, Davy, Arthur, Silas, Fred, Lem, Dessie and I will travel to Louisville with Star and Graceful Lady. Fred and Davy will stay at Churchill Downs with the fillies, while the rest of us will lodge at the Brown Hotel, as usual. I know you will be listening by radio and will be with us in spirit, but now, let's have some music."

She gestured toward a clearing and a small group of men clutching banjos and fiddles. As the music began, I turned to my brother.

"I'm going to grab a jacket, Lem."

He nodded. I headed off and cut through the honeysuckle-vine arbor on the west side of the manor house. I was daydreaming about my first stay in a hotel when I stopped short at the sound of low voices nearby.

"There's the band startin' up. Mr. Hawthorne said to wait until the fifth song to take the black horse from the third stall."

My heart leaped into my throat as I realized the men were talking about Star.

"What do we do about the guard?"

"Mr. Hawthorne said his inside man would take care of him."

The second voice spoke again. "What if the horse puts up a ruckus?"

"Nobody'll hear with that band playin'. One way or another, that horse is goin' in the trailer and will never be seen again."

The men laughed. I slowly backed away, my thoughts swirling. Why would Mr. Hawthorne, who had seemed so nice, want to steal Star? And who was the inside man? As I tried to steady my nerves and decide what to do, I heard applause and realized a song had ended. Was that the first or the second? I didn't have much time if I was going to save Star.

I turned and left the vines, running in an arc away from the men but toward Stable Hall. Moonlight shone through the open door. I tiptoed in and saw Andy lying on the ground. I rushed to his side and felt his chest. He was still breathing but out cold. I saw no injury and figured he had been drugged somehow. I couldn't help Andy further, so I headed to the horse stalls. Star greeted me with a pleased whinny.

I let out the breath I'd been holding and patted her. "Please, Star, be quiet. There are bad men comin'. I'll get you out though. Trust me, okay?"

I bridled her and led her to an empty stall. Then I went into the stall where placid Danny Boy stood quietly munching hay. Luckily he was a black horse, too, although he didn't have the white star on his face. I hoped that bit of information had not been shared by Mr. Hawthorne.

"Hi, Danny Boy. I'm sorry about this, but I need you to come with me." He followed me into Star's empty stall and resumed eating. I took Star's saddle and saddle blanket and hurried back to her. I had just closed the stall door when I heard footsteps. I ducked below the half door. Star seemed to understand and turned her distinctive white star away from the door.

The men skulked by and entered the stall where Danny Boy waited. I hoped they would not be able to tell a black gelding from a black filly, and my luck held. The men led the horse through the side door of Stable Hall. I followed and peeked out. Two men I didn't recognize loaded Danny Boy into the back of a horse trailer attached to a truck. As it sped down the lane, I made a wish that they would not harm Danny Boy.

I rushed to Star and quickly saddled her. "Sorry, girl, but you'll have to make do with me tonight," I said. We left the building, and I turned her in the opposite direction the truck had taken. I kicked Star's flanks, and we galloped across the fields west of the manor house. I remembered the night I'd first ridden Star and was glad there was no rain.

Just when I thought we had missed our destination in the dark, a building loomed ahead. "Oh, thank goodness," I sighed. I pulled Star to a stop and climbed down. I opened the door to the empty tobacco barn and led her inside. She nuzzled my pockets.

"Sorry, girl, no treats. You'll be okay here for a while. I'll come back soon and bring sugar too."

Star began nibbling at loose hay on the floor while I headed back to the party.

***

Around twenty minutes later, I neared the party. Mr. and Miz Hawthorne were the only ones still seated at the head table with Miz Emily.

I approached Miz Emily and whispered in her ear, "Ma'am, can I speak to you, please?"

"Why, Destiny, where have you been?" Miz Emily's voice boomed out, and I wondered if she'd been sampling the moonshine or something like it.

"I need to speak with you in private," I said quietly, feeling Mr. Hawthorne's sharp eyes on me.

"Nonsense. Anything you have to say to me you can say in front of Josiah and Hester. They're old and dear friends." She waved grandly and smiled at them. The Hawthornes nodded, grinning. "What is it, dear?"

She called me an endearment? Now I was sure she'd been tippling.

"I wanted to say what a grand party this is," I said.

Miz Emily patted my arm. "Thank you, Dessie. Run along and get some sleep. We have a big day tomorrow, you know."

"I'll get Lem and we'll go right to bed. Goodnight." She nodded vaguely and turned back to her friends.

I hurried to Lem and noticed that Fred was missing too.

"What took you so long?" Lem asked.

"I need to talk to you. In private." I gestured with my head for him to follow.

He eyed me quizzically but immediately joined me in the vine arbor. I quickly and quietly told him what had happened.

"We should tell Davy. He'll know what to do."

Lem groaned. "We can't. An emergency call came for Doc Wheeler from Calumet. Davy and Fred went along to help."

"That's at least five miles away!"

"I know. Let's tell Miz Emily."

"I tried. She's tipsy, plus those Hawthornes are stuck to her side and he's the one behind this."

Lem's eyes widened in surprise. "Who else can we trust?"

"I don't know. I think Silas Dimkins is Mr. Hawthorne's inside man, but I guess I have no proof," I said grudgingly.

"What about Tobias?"

"We can trust him, of course, but he'd want Miz Emily's approval first and there's no time." I came to a decision. "Lem, you go stay with Star while I get supplies. If anyone comes for her, you can ride away much faster than I could. I'll leave a note for Davy with Tobias and then join you."

"All right, but be careful. That inside man is around somewhere."

He hugged me and headed toward the tobacco barn. I turned the other way and quietly returned to Stable Hall. Andy was still there, sleeping peacefully. I hurried to our room and changed from skirt to overalls. I stuffed two saddlebags with extra clothes, candles, matches and food. In Davy's room, I scrawled a note and sealed it in an envelope. At the last moment, I added three items to my pockets: Davy's detailed state map, Pap's knife and the letter about my poem.

I hurried to Graceful Lady's stall. She greeted me softly.

"Hi, girl. We're goin' to meet Lem and Star." She stood still while I saddled her and tossed the saddlebags over her back. "I'll be back soon," I told her.

I ran to the manor house and tiptoed through the quiet rooms looking for Tobias. I found him tidying Miz Emily's study.

"Hello there. Why, Miss Dessie, what's wrong?"

"Tobias, I need you to do me a favor."

"Of course. Sit down and calm yourself first."

I waved away his concern. "I'm sorry but there's no time." I held out the envelope. "Please have Davy read this as soon as he returns. And make sure no one else is around when he does, okay?"

My friend nodded. "Is there anything else?"

I was halfway out the door. "I almost forgot. Please go see to Andy. He's in Stable Hall. He's been drugged, I think."

With those startling parting words, I hurried back to Lady. I mounted and steered her out of the building and toward the tobacco barn. I took a winding route in case anyone was watching. Each extra second was an agony of anxiety.

When I reached the barn, I halted Lady and called out softly, "Lem, you there?"

The door opened slowly, and I let out a small shriek of relief when a shaft of moonlight caught his silvery hair. "Dess! It's about time you showed up."

"How's Star?"

"She's fine. No one's come around."

"Good. Now mount up. We need to get movin'."

"Where to?"

"To Louisville. We're takin' the horses to the Derby!"

Chapter Sixteen

Lem tried to argue, but I was determined. So he fetched Star and we headed out through the back fields of Rutledge Farms. When we reached the edge of Miz Emily's property, we came to a dirt road. We stopped the horses so I could light a candle and examine Davy's map.

"Dess, you do know that Louisville is at least sixty miles away, right?"

"Yep. We've got five days. Can we make it in time if we ride at night and sleep during the day?"

Lem sighed. "We should be able to do that with time to spare *if* the horses get enough rest and water and *if* we don't get lost."

I shook the map. "That's what this is for. According to the map, this back road will take us through Anderson and Shelby Counties, but when we reach Jefferson County, we'll need to veer south a bit before we enter the city."

"How are we goin' to get into Churchill once we get there?"

"I haven't figured that part out yet."

He sighed again but turned Star to follow Lady as we headed west.

Traveling at night was a bit tricky, but whenever we came to a junction, we stopped and consulted Davy's map. We also had the advantage of seeing headlights in time to move out of sight, which thankfully didn't happen very often. We rode the rest of the night and the next two nights, stopping only when the sun rose. Our luck held, and we were able to find places where we could hide and sleep during the daytime. Twice we stayed in old barns, and on the third day, we holed up in an empty warehouse on the outskirts of Louisville. By then we were both saddle sore and cranky.

Lem took the afternoon watch while I slept. He woke me at dusk, and we ate biscuits while the horses grazed the small patch of grass outside. It had rained earlier, and Lem had collected rainwater in an old barrel. As we ate, we discussed our plans.

"Tell me again what you wrote Davy in the note," said Lem.

I rolled my eyes but did as he asked. "I told Davy about the men taking Danny Boy instead of Star and that she was safe with us. I told him to trust only Tobias and Miz Emily and to meet us at Churchill. And I asked him to use a decoy horse so the thieves would think Star was still at Rutledge."

"Where exactly will we meet them at Churchill?"

"Heck, Lem, I don't know since I've never been there before. You're the horse expert. You tell me what we should do."

He ignored my sarcasm. "I reckon the stables will be in the back."

"Alright. You sleep a while, and I'll get you up in a few hours. The best time for us to sneak through town will be in the middle of the night."

Five hours later, we slowly rode the horses into the city limits. It was eerie, riding through dark and empty streets, knowing that all around people were sleeping the night away. We were as quiet as possible. Before mounting, Lem had wrapped rags around the horses' hooves to deaden the sound when they hit the pavement.

Since I didn't want to stop to consult the map, I had spent the time while Lem was napping memorizing our route. As we got closer, we could see the racetrack's twin spires jutting into the moonlit sky. I used them as a beacon as I navigated through side streets and winding back alleys, keeping us away from the main streets. Eventually, we neared the racetrack and made our way to a back gate.

I was internally congratulating myself on getting us to Churchill without being stopped when Lem let loose with a cuss word.

"What's wrong?" I whispered.

"The gate's locked." He nodded at the heavy chain and padlock joining the bars of the tall white gate before us. "I guess we'll have to wait until mornin'."

I pulled out Pap's knife and slid to the ground. I didn't want to wait anymore. I marched up to the lock, stuck the knifepoint in and jiggled it around.

"Dess, stop that. You can't unlock it that way."

"Hey there! What are you doin'?" a man's voice yelled. Light suddenly flooded the scene. I dropped the lock and stepped back in surprise. A man stood behind the gate holding a lantern high. I was thinking up an answer when the man began to laugh. The light blinded me, but I recognized that laugh.

"Mr. Red, is that you?" I asked incredulously. "Are you the night watchman?"

He stopped laughing and lowered the lantern. "Yep, Dessie, I am. What in blue blazes are you and Lem doin' here?"

"We've brought Star of Destiny to race in the Derby."

"You've what?" He looked at Lem still sitting on Star. "Is that really the Rutledge horse?"

Lem smiled and patted Star. "Yep. It's a long story, but if you'll let us in, we'll tell you."

Mr. Red pulled out a ring of keys. He unlocked the gate and opened it wide. He started to lead us to the stables where the Thoroughbreds stayed, but I shook my head, and he took us instead to an empty barn at the rear of the track property.

While we unsaddled the horses and brushed them down, Mr. Red brought two buckets with feed for Star and Graceful Lady. He turned over another bucket and sat down to hear our story. We took turns telling him all that had happened since we'd parted at the train station.

"So you see, we won't be sure that Star is safe until we can hand her over to Davy."

Mr. Red stroked his chin with one big hand. "You kids didn't have any trouble at all on the way here?"

"Not a bit, other than Dessie turnin' the map upside down once or twice," joked Lem.

"Hmm, it seems strange that Hawthorne didn't send anyone to follow you. The story around here is that Star of Destiny is ill and will be scratched from the race, but Miz Rutledge hasn't done it yet. She brought a couple of her men to town with her, but she's holed up at the Brown, fending off the press and the race officials. Davy Shaw is supposed to come in tomorrow with the horse."

"So Davy has been pretendin' he's still got Star. That's why we weren't followed," I said.

"Could be. Or could be that Hawthorne has a backup plan. Well, we can't worry about that now. You need some sleep. I guess you want to stay here?" We nodded. "Alright then. Blankets are in the corner. I'll go on my rounds, but I'll check on you at first light."

I gave our friend a hug. "Thank you, Mr. Red. You've come through for us again."

He patted my back. "I guess there was a reason I didn't get to St. Louis after all."

I awoke at dawn to a strong call of nature. I rose and tiptoed out of the stall and barn, looking for a privy I could use in this place dominated by men. Luckily, I found what I needed near the jockeys' quarters and sneaked in and out without being seen.

I retraced my steps, feeling lighthearted and breathing deeply of the sweet early morning air. I turned the corner of the building and jumped back to avoid two men I knew. Arthur Reed and Fred Newsom were walking in my direction. I looked around for a place to hide and ducked

behind a wooden bench as they rounded the corner.

"Here, Fred, stop a moment."

I heard the sound of a match being struck and realized they were

lighting cigarettes. I made myself as still and silent as I could.

"What's the plan, Mr. Reed?" Fred asked.

"I just got a call from Hawthorne. Jeb told him that Davy and Tobias

loaded a horse in a trailer a few minutes ago, but it's not Star. So the

supposedly sick horse that Davy's been nursing in private is a decoy, and

Rutledge is going to have to scratch. You aren't needed any longer. I've

got your money and a train ticket out of town."

"That's fine by me, but what if those kids show up with the right horse

after all?"

Mr. Reed laughed. "That's the real Derby long shot! But if they do,

there won't be a jockey to ride Star, will there?"

Fred chuckled, and after a moment when I supposed money was

changing hands, they walked on. I bit my tongue to keep from shouting

at their retreating backs. Jeb, Mr. Reed and Fred! Hawthorne's spies

were all over Rutledge! But Fred was the worst; Davy had trusted him. I

hurried back to Lem and the horses.

I found Lem awake and talking with Mr. Red. I quickly told them what I'd heard.

"I need to go see Miz Emily. Mr. Red, how can I get to the Brown Hotel?"

"It's about three miles from here, Dessie, but you should take the trolley." He noticed my hesitation, dug in his pocket and held out a handful of coins. "Take this."

"Thank you again. I'll pay you back as soon as I can. Do you think Lem and the horses will be safe here?"

"My shift is over, so I'll nap here today. But let me take you out the back gate so you don't run into that Mr. Reed."

"That'll work. Lem, I'll bring Miz Emily. She'll find a new jockey for Star. Don't give up now when we're this close." Lem nodded and gave me a thumbs-up.

Half an hour later, I was ushered through the double door and up two short flights of stairs at the Brown Hotel by a disapproving doorman. I glanced down and realized I was still wearing dirty overalls. I looked up, and my mouth dropped open. I was entering a huge room with walls that seemed to be a hundred feet tall. Floor-to-ceiling columns lined the center of the room, and a series of intricately carved archways stood parallel to the columns. Huge ferns and overstuffed furniture were scattered throughout the lobby. Well-dressed people filled the sofas and stood talking in groups. I made my way to a desk under one of the archways.

"May I help you?" asked the pretty girl behind the counter.

"Yes, I need the room number for Emily Rutledge, please."

"Mrs. Rutledge has asked to not be disturbed."

"She'll want to see me." I cast around for a reason. "I'm her granddaughter."

"Oh really?" the girl asked doubtfully.

I snatched off my cap, and my curls tumbled down. "See? I'm a girl."

"Do you have proof you are a relative of Mrs. Rutledge's?"

"Of course not. I guess I'll go look for myself." I started to turn away, but she put a hand on my arm.

"Only patrons of the hotel are allowed upstairs."

I slapped my hands to my thighs in frustration and felt paper crinkle. "But I am a patron." I pulled out my letter and shoved it toward the girl. "Here, read this."

She unfolded the letter and read it silently while I counted the seconds. "This says you will be staying with an adult. Where is your companion?"

I was fed up with her snooty attitude. "My companion is busy at the moment. He'll be here later."

"Only an adult may register. Next!"

I snatched my letter back and turned away dejectedly. I spied an empty chair across the lobby and sank into it. My eyes met those of a young man seated across from me. I didn't recognize the fancy clothes he wore, but I recognized those green eyes.

"You rat-fink! Look at you, all dressed up. Did you buy those clothes with my money?!"

"Shh, girl. Please don't make a scene," said Brendan Cole.

"I'll do more than that. I'll find a policeman and get you arrested."

"Dessie, I'm sorry I stole from you, but I was starving and desperate." Brendan gave me a sorrowful look.

"So you do remember me? What I remember is that you're a liar."

"Look, lower your voice and tell me what I can do to make it up to you. You want your money back? Here's ten dollars. That's more than I took, so we're even." He tossed the bill at me and started to rise.

"Not so fast," I said as I pocketed the bill. "I could still turn you in. Do one more thing for me and I'll let you go."

He eyed me warily. "What thing?"

I grabbed his arm and pulled him toward the reception desk. "I don't have time to explain. Just follow my lead," I whispered.

"Here's my adult companion," I announced to the girl behind the desk. She looked at Brendan, and her eyes opened wide. "Give me a room, now."

Brendan didn't let me down. He leaned on the counter and winked at the girl. "Aren't little sisters a pain? Mine insists on wearing overalls even though she has a closet full of dresses."

"Y-y-yes. Mine is the same, at home that is. Uhm, sign the register and I'll get your key."

"Sign Lemuel Soames," I hissed as she turned away.

The girl asked to see my letter again to show the manager. She returned it to Brendan, but I snatched away the key. He held the letter up and read it as we crossed the lobby and entered the elevator.

"A free room at the Brown! Perhaps I should take up poetry."

"Give me the letter and you can have the key. I don't need the room."

"What's the catch?" he asked suspiciously.

"No catch. I need to find Emily Rutledge of Rutledge Farms," I sighed.

"I can help you there. She's in room 415."

I smiled happily at this news as we traded but then remembered he was a rat-fink. "Is that a lie?"

"No lie." He crossed his heart and grinned. Despite good intentions to stay angry, I smiled back.

"Here's my floor," he said. The elevator doors opened. Brendan winked at me as he left. "Say hello to the lieutenant governor, sis."

"I hope I never see you again!" I yelled and heard his laughter as the elevator climbed to the next floor.

I rushed out and hurried to Miz Emily's room. I banged on the door until I heard footsteps. The door jerked open, and I was face to face with Arthur Reed.

"Dessie!"

I rushed past him to the woman seated by the window. "Miz Emily."

"Destiny, child. Where have you been?"

"I have so much to tell you." I stopped short, remembering we were not alone. "Mr. Reed, I'm awful hungry. Would you get me a ham sandwich?"

"Of course, my dear. I'll order room service."

I forced myself to smile. "I'm very allergic to mustard. Won't you go make sure they fix it right? Please?"

"Yes, do go, Arthur." Miz Emily waved him away, and he had no choice.

I peeked out to make sure he was gone and then rushed to tell Miz Emily all that had happened and about the conversation I'd overheard.

"I can't believe that Josiah is behind all this," she said for the tenth time.

"Mr. Reed is in it too," I reminded her, "and he'll be back soon. We need to get to the track."

"You're right, of course. Let's go."

Miz Emily led me down the hall to another set of elevators and out a side door. She raised her cane, and a taxi drew up in seconds. When we arrived at Churchill a few minutes later, we found Davy waiting for a taxi of his own to take to the Brown. I was so happy to see him that I hugged him twice.

Miz Emily found the track manager, who provided a car to take us to the barn where Lem waited with Mr. Red and the horses. After introducing Mr. Red, Lem filled Davy in on everything. He listened in grim silence until Lem got to the part about Fred.

"Ooh-ee, I'd never have guessed he'd take payola."

"Davy, can you find another jockey by tomorrow?" asked Miz Emily hopefully.

"We've been tryin'. Silas realized this mornin' that Fred had skipped. He made the rounds here, but everybody's got a mount for the Derby. He was goin' to come find you when I showed up." Davy pulled out his pouch and began filling his pipe. "I don't believe Silas is workin' for Hawthorne. You should have seen his face when he found Diamond Girl instead of Star in the trailer. You can't fake that kind of shock."

Davy chuckled while I grudgingly struck Silas Dimkins off my list of suspects. "We could make some calls, Emily, but I don't know how Star would do with a strange jockey. I'd hate for you to pay the expense and she just bucks him off."

Everyone regarded Star. She stood placidly eating hay, but we knew how easily she could throw a rider if riled.

Miz Emily sighed. "I guess that's it. I'll go to the clubhouse and scratch Star from the Derby. Then I'll take Lem and Dessie to the hotel to get cleaned up."

"No," I said.

"Now young lady, I don't know why you hate bathing so much, but this has got to stop."

"I'll be glad to take a bath, Miz Emily, but don't scratch Star. We have the perfect jockey." I pointed and Star nodded her agreement, in spite of the storm of protest that broke around us.

Chapter Seventeen

"Lem can do it," I said stubbornly for the twentieth time. I ticked off the reasons. "He's old enough. Star likes him. Besides, his trial times were faster than Fred's."

"Is that true, Davy?" I saw the gleam in Miz Emily's eyes.

Davy frowned at me. "Aye," he said, grudgingly.

Miz Emily turned to my brother, who had remained silent. "Lemuel, you don't have to do this. You are young and inexperienced, and horse racing is dangerous. What do you say?"

"I understand the danger, but I want to race Star in the Derby. It'll be a dream come true," he said, his eyes shining.

"Perhaps for all of us," said Miz Emily, surprising Lem with a hug. She looked surprised herself and quickly stepped away to issue orders.

"Excuse me, Miz Emily," interrupted Lem.

"Yes, what now?"

"Since I'll be ridin' Star, I think she'd be fine with Davy on Lady. That way, Dessie can meet the lieutenant governor before he reads her poem to the crowd."

It was my turn to protest. Lem smiled serenely as he explained about me winning the contest. Miz Emily was pleased as punch but stared at me, aghast.

"Destiny, your clothes! After we see Star and Lady safely settled, we are going shopping. You cannot meet Happy Chandler in dirty overalls!"

***

The fifty-ninth Run for the Roses found our team bleary-eyed but ready. Davy, Mr. Red and Silas had taken turns guarding the horses through the night while Lem and I grabbed a few hours of sleep on sofas in Miz Emily's suite. After breakfast, Lem dressed in the purple and white silks while I put on the blue and white dress we had bought.

"Destiny, do stand still while I brush your hair. Perhaps a bow…" She noticed my face and added, "Or perhaps not. That will have to do." Her expression softened. "I mean, you will do nicely."

Once at Churchill, we learned that Arthur Reed had been seen catching an outbound train the previous evening. Miz Emily gave last instructions to Davy as I said goodbye to Lem.

I gave him a hug. "Good luck, Lem. You and Star will do great!"

"Thanks, Dess. I wouldn't be here if it weren't for you."

Miz Emily turned to Lem while I hugged Davy and patted the horses. Then she dragged me to the car waiting to take us to the main entrance. As we made our way to the Rutledge box, I looked around at my surroundings. My heart lifted at the sight of the familiar twin spires atop the grandstand. We crossed the garden area between the main gate and the grandstand where men in suits and women in pastel dresses gathered around white benches. I fidgeted impatiently whenever Miz Emily stopped to chat. The Rutledge box was in the upper tier of the grandstand. Miz Emily doggedly climbed to the box, which could easily have seated a half dozen, and then settled herself grandly into her seat. She gazed around at the other boxes, but I only had eyes for the brown oval below.

"We're too far up," I complained. "Lem and Star will look like ants from here."

Miz Emily opened her reticule and removed two objects. "These are opera glasses, Destiny." She handed one set to me and held the other to her eyes. I copied her and was amazed at how closely I could see faraway objects. I trained them on the race below and was able to bring even the jockeys' faces into focus. I scanned the pleasant view before me, studying the lengths and curves of the track, the grassy infield, and the board for posting race results. I eventually found the winner's presentation stand near the clubhouse.

In between races, I amused myself by scanning the crowd that was growing in the infield across from us, many already leaning on the inside rail of the track. My companion trained her opera glasses on the rich and famous around us. She murmured names and commentary under her breath about people she recognized. "Edith Wilson, James Roosevelt, Postmaster Farley; D.C. is well represented. Where are the locals? Ah, the Masons and the Coes are here, and of course, Agnes and the Colonel."

"The Colonel?" I asked.

"Colonel E.R. Bradley, the first owner to win three times," said Miz Emily. "He owns Brokers Tip. The Colonel is quite a character. He first predicted that Ladysman will win the Derby, but this morning, he stated that his horse will win." She winked at me. "Let's hope Star and Lem make the Colonel wrong on both counts."

As I smiled back, my stomach growled. Miz Emily summoned a waiter and ordered sandwiches for two. These were soon delivered on a tray, along with lemonade for me and a drink called a mint julep for Miz Emily. She took a sip and grimaced, saying, "It's just not the same without bourbon."

I was finishing my sandwich, my attention on a claims race, when I heard a familiar and unwelcome voice.

"Good afternoon, Emily," boomed Josiah Hawthorne. "Hester and I apologize for keeping you waiting." He started forward as though to enter the box. Miz Emily stood and blocked his way, causing Miz Hawthorne to bump into her husband's back with a surprised squeal.

"Why, what's wrong? You did invite us to share your box for the Derby, didn't you?"

"I may have," she said firmly, "but that was before I knew you were trying to steal my horse!"

"I don't know what you are talking about, I assure you," he replied smoothly, but I noticed his forehead starting to sweat. Conversations stopped around us.

"You sent men to steal Star the night of the party at Rutledge," I chimed in.

"That's nonsense. Surely, Emily, you don't believe the lies of this child over my word. We've been friends for years."

"Yes, years," echoed Miz Hawthorne vaguely.

"I do believe her. Not only did you try to steal Star, but you drugged one of my men, bribed our jockey and I suspect you caused Prince's accident too!"

Mr. Hawthorne chuckled. "Do I also cause floods and famines? Come now, you must know how ridiculous you sound. It is certainly not my fault that you can't keep a jockey and that your horse is too ill to run the race."

Miz Emily smiled, and I almost felt sorry for what was about to hit Mr. Hawthorne. "Now who is being ridiculous, Josiah? Nine horses were scratched this morning, but Star wasn't one of them. You would know that if your henchman, Arthur Reed, hadn't high-tailed it out of town yesterday."

Mr. Hawthorne's pasty face turned even whiter. "Why…that's wonderful news about your horse. I'm…not feeling well. Do let us sit down."

Miz Emily stamped her cane. "Not in my box you don't. You've been after me to sell Rutledge ever since J.L. died. I guess you decided to try to force me to do so."

Josiah Hawthorne's voice turned mean. "You can't treat me like this. Don't forget who I am, Emily. You have no proof against me. I could sue for slander."

"I would say that three eyewitnesses to Star's attempted abduction is proof, Josiah. You may sue me if you wish, but I advise you to leave Kentucky quickly. Now, step aside. We have an appointment with the lieutenant governor."

Mr. Hawthorne backed away, mopping his brow as we passed. Miz Emily paused, calling back, "Oh, and do stop the fake swooning, Hester."

I dissolved in giggles and almost tripped down the stairs. Safely at the bottom, I gave Miz Emily a quick hug, startling her.

"Destiny!"

"You were wonderful. I don't think Mr. Hawthorne knew you were bluffing at all."

"I never bluff; everyone knows that."

"Oh." Before I had time to decide if she was joking or not, we were climbing the steps to the winner's presentation box, and I was introduced to the lieutenant governor.

Happy Chandler greeted me enthusiastically, holding my hand after shaking it and gazing into my eyes. "Hello there, Destiny," he said. "I am so very pleased to meet the girl who wrote this excellent poem. I am honored to read it to the state and the world."

"The world?" I gulped.

Mr. Chandler's face split into a wide grin. "Yep," he whispered loudly, "we're *international*." He pointed to the radio announcer and microphone stand. My legs felt like spaghetti noodles as Mr. Chandler began his address. He welcomed the crowd and the radio audience to the Derby and shared a message from the governor. Then he spoke briefly about the statewide contest and introduced me.

"The winning poem was written by Destiny Rose Soames. Destiny hails from the fine town of Whitburn and is the daughter of Calton and Lillian Soames. Destiny's poem was submitted by her teacher, Susannah Morrisey. Her poem is titled 'My Blue Kentucky.'"

As Happy Chandler read my poem into the microphone, I stood tall and gazed into the crowd. I knew Lem and Davy were with the horses, ready to circle the paddock, but I hoped they could hear. When he ended, the crowd erupted into applause.

"Wasn't that just dandy? Well done, Destiny!" Mr. Chandler clapped me on the back. "Now, let's stand and sing 'My Old Kentucky Home.'" He gestured widely, and the crowd stood. Miz Emily steered me toward our box for the start of the race. I glanced back and received a wink and a grin from the lieutenant governor.

We hurried past well-wishers and arrived in time to see Lem and Star in the parade to the starting gate, led by Davy and Graceful Lady. Lem held the reins tightly and kept his eyes down, unlike the other jockeys, who waved and called to the crowd.

Fourteen horses were led into the starting gate. I watched through my opera glasses and was relieved that Star didn't balk at all.

The gate doors opened, and they were off! Like number sixteen, Brokers Tip, Star started slowly. Both quickly gained ground as the field, led by number eleven, Head Play, raced past the stands the first time and on around the clubhouse turn. Brokers Tip was running on the inside, with Star next to him, staying neck and neck. Together, they passed several other horses and, by the far turn, were gaining on the leaders.

At the top of the stretch, Head Play suddenly swerved outside. Head Play's jockey swerved him back on track while Star and Colonel Bradley's horse shot forward. Head Play and Brokers Tip pounded down the track, with Star hemmed in between them but slightly behind, while space lengthened between the leading three horses and the rest of the field.

I held my breath, sure that Star would fall back, afraid to push through the gap. Lem dug his heels into her flanks, and she nudged forward. I cheered joyfully. Just then, Head Play dropped toward the inside, closer to his rival. The jockey riding Brokers Tip thrust his hand out toward Head Play. Star reacted immediately. She slowed and reared back, whinnying loudly. When she came down on all hooves, the shock was so great that it sent Lem flying over her head. He landed violently and lay still, his arms and legs splayed. Brokers Tip and Head Play continued on down the track, their jockeys locked in a bizarre struggle, each grabbing at the other over the backs of their mounts.

"Lem!" I screamed. I looked fearfully at the pack of horses pounding toward his motionless body.

Suddenly, a man vaulted over the rail from the infield. He struck Star on her flank, sending her bolting out of harm's way. I got a look at his face before he turned toward Lem.

"Pap! Miz Emily, its Pap!"

Pap scooped Lem up in his arms and dashed back toward the rail. He handed him over to a man waiting there whom I recognized as Silas Dimkins. Pap hesitated for a moment, glancing at the advancing field of horses. As he started to climb over the rail, the pack reached him, and the rider closest to the rail clipped Pap, vaulting him head-first into the infield. I lost sight of where he was, so tight was the crowd of railbirds.

"I have to get to Lem and Pap!" I pushed past Miz Emily and fled down the steps. A guard stopped me when I tried to cross the track, but Mr. Red suddenly materialized and escorted me across. Out of the corner of my eye, I caught a flash of red. It was the garland of red roses being draped over the neck of Brokers Tip in the winner's circle. Later I would learn that the fighting finish of the race had so transfixed the crowd that my family's drama went largely unnoticed. By the time I arrived, most of the infield crowd had left to gather near the winning horse.

Mr. Red lifted me over the rail, and I hurried to where Lem and Pap lay. Silas Dimkins held Lem's head in his lap. Lem was unconscious, but his chest rose and fell in a steady rhythm, and I sagged in relief.

I turned to Pap. He lay so still—unnaturally still. "Pap!" I cried and flung myself on his chest. "Oh, Pap." One part of my brain knew he was gone, but another part of my brain resisted. I lost track of time as I lay sobbing and clinging to my father. Eventually, I felt strong hands gently pull me away, and I turned into Davy's arms.

"There now, lass. I'm so very sorry." He held me and patted me softly until I pulled back when two ambulances arrived.

Miz Emily handed me her lace handkerchief. "Here, my dear." I wiped my face as the attendants loaded Pap and Lem. "Come, Dessie. We'll go to the hospital. You'll be there when Lem wakes up."

I turned back as we were leaving. "Davy?"

"Go now. I'll see to Star."

***

At the hospital, Miz Emily left me while she went to ask about Lem. I was sent to wait in a white ugly room with cracking paint. I wondered idly how they could fix people if they couldn't fix their walls. I paced back and forth. I guess I was afraid that if I sat down, the truth would catch up with me and I'd know for certain that Pap was dead.

"Destiny, please stop pacing. That won't help Lem," said Miz Emily as she returned.

"Maybe it helps me," I muttered.

"Excuse me?"

"I said, maybe you could talk to me."

"Talking would be good," Miz Emily said uncertainly. "Is there anything I can get you, anything you want?"

"I want my mother. I want Mam."

"She'll be here tomorrow."

"How do you know that?" I asked incredulously.

"I just sent her a telegram saying Lem was hurt, and I wired her money for train tickets and taxis."

"You didn't tell her about Pap." Miz Emily shook her head. "Why not?"

Miz Emily did then what I never expected. She started crying. "There's something you don't know. You see, your mother is my daughter. I couldn't let her find out about Calton in a telegram."

"Thank you...Grandmother," I said. I was too tired and too heartsick about Lem and Pap to fuss at her for not telling me sooner.

"Oh, Dessie, I love you and Lem very much. I'm sorry I didn't say so until now." She opened her arms and folded me into her embrace.

By the time the doctor came to talk to us, Davy, Silas and Mr. Red had joined us. The doctor came right to the point.

"I have good news, folks. Lemuel suffered a concussion and two broken ribs, but he'll be fine. He's conscious and anxious for visitors."

The doctor turned sober. "He doesn't know yet what happened after he fell. You'll need to break it to him gently."

"Thank you, Dr. Turner. We understand."

Miz Emily took my hand. "Do you want me to talk to Lem alone first?"

I shook my head. "No. I'm the one closest to Lem. It's me who brought him here, and it's my fault he raced. I'll tell him, but I'd like you to be there."

She smiled and pushed a curl away from my forehead, and I fleetingly thought that was a grandmotherly thing to do as we entered Lem's room.

His head and chest were bandaged and dark circles ringed his eyes, but he smiled when he saw us.

"Dess, Miz Emily. I'm sorry about losin'."

"Lemuel, you have nothing to be sorry about," said Miz Emily brusquely. "You could not have anticipated those two fool jockeys flailing at each other and startling Star."

"Is Star hurt?" he asked, and I shook my head.

"Star's fine, Lem."

"How did I get off the track? I don't remember anythin' that happened once I flew over her head."

I sat down in a chair near the bed and looked into Lem's dear face. "It was Pap, Lem. I don't know why he was there, but he ran out of the crowd and saved you."

"Pap? I don't understand." Lem looked toward the door. "Where is he?"

"He got hurt tryin' to get off the track. Davy says Pap hit his head on the rail when he fell."

"So he's in another room?" I shook my head again, and the truth dawned in Lem's eyes. "But I hit my head and I'm all right."

"I know, but it wasn't that way for Pap. Davy says he went real quick, without pain."

"I can't believe it." Lem looked dazed.

Our grandmother spoke softly. "Your father must have loved his children very much."

Lem looked at me. "Do you reckon so, Dess?"

"I've been mad at Pap a long time, but I never really thought he didn't love us. He just didn't show it much."

"Not until today."

I reached out and squeezed my brother's hand. "Not until today, Lem. He sure showed it today."

***

The next day, Mam arrived at the hospital. I grabbed her as she climbed out of the taxi, repeating over and over that I was sorry. She pulled back and looked at me in confusion.

"Dessie, honey, I got the second telegram so I know Lem's better. You don't have to apologize." She stroked my hair, and I gulped back the words I was going to say about Pap. My grandmother had asked to let her tell Mam.

Miz Emily came forward. "Lillian, dear, I've missed you so." She held out her arms, and my surprised mother went into her embrace. "Oh, Mama, I've missed you too."

C.J. bellowed from the taxi. I rushed forward to hold him, hiding my streaming face in his silken hair. Silas Dimkins suddenly appeared and lifted Emmie out of the car. It was so strange to hear him babble baby talk that my tears dried instantly.

As we entered the hospital, Mam asked, "Is Calton with Lem? He was so determined to come after Ms. Evelyn mentioned that her sister Hester said you two had stolen horses from Rutledge. Cal said he'd prove your innocence if it was the last thing he did."

I only managed a strangled, "Davy's with Lem."

"Lillian, we need to talk before you see Lemuel." Miz Emily steered Mam to a quiet corner of the waiting room while Silas and I settled down across the way with the babies. Silas pulled out his watch and a wad of keys for them to play with.

I couldn't hear what was said, but I watched Mam's face. I saw her expression turn from confusion to disbelief to grief. She didn't sob as I had done but sat like stone, holding tightly to my grandmother's hand. They stayed that way for a long time, and I wondered if they were remembering their other, older grief, too. Eventually, they rose and walked slowly toward Lem's room.

Pap's funeral was held three days later. Miz Emily insisted that he be buried in the family cemetery at Rutledge. In spite of how he'd been blackballed years before, dozens of horse racing folks came to pay their respects. Mr. and Miz Hawthorne were missing, of course, but I saw many familiar faces from the Bluegrass Breeders' Syndicate. Even Mr. Baker who had criticized Pap that day at the syndicate office was there.

Lem was there too. Mam held on tight to him throughout the service. Even though he was still bruised and bandaged, it seemed to me that my brother had grown up overnight. He stood straighter and spoke with a new firmness in his voice I hardly recognized.

After the last mourner left, Miz Emily gathered our family in her study. She asked Davy to join us and directed Tobias and Margaret to watch the babies. She handed me a glass of lemonade and passed around glasses of wine to the others.

"Why, Emily, are you defyin' Prohibition?"

"Yes, Davy, I am. I think we adults deserve a little fortification after what we've been through the past few days. Don't you agree, Lem?"

He looked up, surprised. "Yes, ma'am; I mean, yes, Grandmother." He sipped his wine slowly. I started to pout until I noticed his grimace at the taste.

"I asked you all here to make plans. Lillian, I want you and the children to stay and live here with me." Miz Emily's voice grew thick. "You don't know how many times I've regretted sending you away."

My mother stood and gazed at the portrait of her father. "Mama, don't be too quick to apologize until you hear the truth."

"What truth, dear?"

Mam spun to face her mother. "The truth about Johnny's death. You see, Calton didn't start the fire that day. He wasn't drunk and he wasn't smoking, only sleeping. I caused the fire."

No one spoke as she paced back and forth, talking rapidly.

"I was ironing in the kitchen when my neighbor called to me through the window. I rushed out to see her and gossip over the fence. I forgot about the hot iron and stayed too long, I guess, because the next thing I knew, flames and smoke were pouring out the kitchen door."

Mam turned to Miz Emily. "I tried to save Johnny, Mama, but I couldn't. I screamed and banged on the window and woke Cal up. He burned his face and arms trying to get to the front room, but the flames were too strong. Later, after Daddy died, Cal told me the rumors that were going around about him. He took the blame so you wouldn't know that your daughter had killed your son and your husband!"

Mam collapsed sobbing on the sofa. I started toward her, but Davy touched my arm and shook his head. Our grandmother went instead, kneeling by Mam's side and stroking her hair. "Hush, child. We've all made mistakes in life; some long ago, some more recently." She looked at me, and I knew she understood the guilt I felt about the accident at the Derby. "It's time for us to forgive each other and start over."

I nodded and felt the pressure ease around my heart. We would be all right. My family had broken apart, but we would mend and be strong again.

I turned and gazed out the window to the night sky, where the first stars were twinkling. I looked to the right of the full moon and found my wishing star. "Thank you, Pap," I whispered. "Thank you for helping us find our way home."

Readers' Guide to

Blue Dust Days

Comprehension Quiz

1. What common Kentucky profession does Calton Soames
   have at the beginning of the story?
   a. Fireman
   b. Coal miner
   c. Factory worker
   d. Mechanic

2. The type of job or profession that a person has is often
   influenced by where he or she lives. Where does the Soames
   family live?
   a. Western Kentucky
   b. Eastern Kentucky
   c. Southern Kentucky
   d. Central Kentucky

3. Part of understanding the plot of a story is knowing about
   the period in which the characters lived. In which period of
   U.S. history does this story take place?
   a. Colonization
   b. Expansion
   c. Depression
   d. Industrialization

4. Why is the Soames family able to move into another house
   so quickly after their house burns?
   a. Harlow Gumbs sells houses as an additional job, so
      Pap makes an offer.
   b. Their family is rich from horse racing, so they use
      family money to buy a new one.
   c. Since the coal mine company owns the houses for
      the miners, they can move.
   d. Miz Hampton loves Lem, so she gives them a house
      down the road from her.

5. What job does Mam do when Pap is injured and unable to work?
   a. Clean the house for Miz Hampton
   b. Make blankets for Verna Gumbs
   c. Sell goods at the company store
   d. Make and sell moonshine

6. Mining companies would partially pay their workers with *scrip*. What is scrip?
   a. Extra money given to those who came in early and worked late
   b. Counterfeit money that could easily fool workers
   c. Coupons given to workers to reduce the cost of goods
   d. Official papers that could be traded for goods in the company store

7. Why is the mine closed the day that Lem gets lost in the mine?
   a. It is a holiday, so they want to give the workers a break to be with their families.
   b. The company closes the mine when it has big stockpiles of coal to save money.
   c. The mine has been shut down for good due to a surplus of coal in West Virginia.
   d. The mine is closed on weekends like the other businesses in the area.

8. Dessie loves her brother and wants him to achieve greatness because he has a great gift. What dream does Lem have for his future?
   a. To be a writer
   b. To go to college
   c. To be a jockey
   d. To be a coal miner

9. Dessie's teacher believes in her writing talent and submitted Dessie's Kentucky poem to a contest. What does Dessie win with her poem?
   a. A paid trip for two to the Kentucky Derby, where it will be read aloud
   b. A paid trip for two to Lexington, where it will be read on the radio
   c. A paid trip for her family to visit the horse farms in Harlow, Kentucky
   d. A paid trip for two to Frankfort, where she will meet the lieutenant governor

10. At the beginning of their trip away from home, Dessie and Lem learn a valuable lesson when they meet Brendan Cole. What happens at the train station as they wait for the train?
    a. Brendan shows them kindness by selling them a nice money pouch.
    b. Brendan helps them plot out their trip and budget their money.
    c. Brendan tricks them into buying a money pouch and steals their money.
    d. Brendan swindles them into selling the brooch Dessie had taken.

11. Dessie and Lem go looking for Davy Shaw at the Bluegrass Breeders' Syndicate office, where they meet Hank, who gives them a ride in the back of his truck to Rutledge Farms. When they arrive, Silas Dimkins lies and tells Dessie and Lem what?
    a. He never knew their father, Calton Soames.
    b. Davy Shaw does not work for Rutledge Farms.
    c. He has never heard of Davy Shaw and to leave immediately.
    d. He doesn't know when Davy Shaw will return to Rutledge Farms.

12. Dessie has proven to be an adventurous young lady but still has some fears. What does Dessie do for the first time to get help for Lem when he is sick?
    a. Jump off a moving train
    b. Drive a car to the doctor
    c. Ride a horse to a nearby house
    d. Try to sell Mam's brooch for money

13. Dessie and Lem seem to make the best of opportunities that come their way. Where do Dessie and Lem spend the night on Lem's birthday?
    a. In a tree house
    b. In a train car
    c. In a barn
    d. In a homeless shelter

14. Dessie develops a special bond with Star of Destiny at Rutledge Farms. What does Dessie learn that she and Star have in common?
    a. They are both orphans.
    b. They have both survived a fire.
    c. They share the same birthday.
    d. Neither one likes Davy Shaw.

15. Dessie had taken her mother's brooch for security in case they ran into trouble and needed money. What is a synonym for the word *brooch*?
    a. Necklace
    b. Pin
    c. Satchel
    d. Purse

16. What does Dessie find that causes her to suspect that Miz Emily is her grandmother?
    a. A brooch
    b. A photograph
    c. A letter
    d. A trophy

17. What does Dessie discover about her parents' lives before she and her siblings were born?
    a. They had lived in Lexington, Kentucky.
    b. Mam's parents own Rutledge Farms.
    c. A fire at their apartment led to the death of Mam's brother.
    d. All of the above

18. What was Pap's profession when he lived in Lexington?
    a. Veterinarian
    b. Coal miner
    c. Horse trainer
    d. Jockey

19. Miz Emily personally sees to Dessie's studies. What subject does Miz Emily insist that Dessie learn to be a proper young lady?
    a. French
    b. Cooking
    c. Manners
    d. Dancing

20. Who does Dessie suspect of being Josiah Hawthorne's inside man causing problems at Rutledge Farms?
    a. Arthur Reed
    b. Silas Dimkins
    c. Davy Shaw
    d. Fred Newsom

21. Which horse is injured at Rutledge Farms and dies before the Derby?
    a. Danny Boy
    b. Star of Destiny
    c. Prince of Egypt
    d. Graceful Lady

22. What does Dessie do to save Star from being kidnapped?
    a. Tells Miz Emily about the plot
    b. Confronts Mr. Hawthorne
    c. Calls the police
    d. Switches Danny Boy for Star in her stall

23. Life has a way of coming full circle sometimes. Who are Dessie and Lem reunited with at Churchill Downs who helps them again?
    a. Mr. Red
    b. Brendan Cole
    c. Verna Gumbs
    d. Arthur Reed

24. Toward the end of the story, Pap proves his love for Lem. What does Pap do to save Lem?
    a. Teaches him how to ride in the Kentucky Derby
    b. Brings the sheriff to arrest Mr. Hawthorne
    c. Catches Lem when he falls off Star during the race
    d. Carries Lem off the track and away from the oncoming riders

25. What secret does Mam reveal after Pap's funeral?
    a. Pap left the family a huge fortune.
    b. Mam had been the one to cause the fire that killed her brother.
    c. Mam and Pap had been planning to move to Lexington before he died.
    d. None of the above

Discussion Questions

1. The Depression had an impact on the growth and development of the United States. Discuss the working conditions for coal miners at the time of the Depression. Consider the following in your details:
   a. hours and days worked
   b. physical labor involved
   c. tools and machinery
   d. physical environment
   e. laws and rules

2. Mining companies controlled much of the businesses and living conditions around their mines. Describe the living conditions for coal mining families at the time of the Depression. Consider the following in your discussion:
   a. housing
   b. transportation
   c. grocery and other stores
   d. plumbing
   e. schools and education
   f. bills and family budgets

3. Recall Dessie and Lem's experiences as the children of a coal miner. Give examples in the story of activities young people did for recreation in Whitburn, as well as chores they were assigned. Compare and contrast their experiences with those of children today.

4. Coal mining is a profession that is often followed by multiple generations of a family. Explain why coal mining is a tradition in many eastern Kentucky families.

5. Dessie shows her knowledge of the land by mapping out her and Lem's escape route. Explain why following the train track was the shortest route out of Whitburn to Hayward.

6. Working conditions have changed throughout U.S. history.
   a. Explain why coal mining companies resisted miners forming unions, sometimes to the point where violence occurred to put down strikes, such as in Harlan County, Kentucky, in the 1930s.
   b. Discuss how unions and strikes are different today than they were in the Depression years.

7. Life can be affected by many factors that influence the decisions that we make.
   a. Discuss some of the reasons that led Dessie to run away with Lem.
   b. What factors affect your decisions?
   c. How is running away from home different today than it was in the 1930s? The same?

8. Miz Emily was slow to acknowledge that Dessie and Lem were her grandchildren.
   a. Do you think that Miz Emily was justified in the decision she made about making her daughter choose between her parents or Calton? Why or why not?
   b. Describe a misunderstanding you have had with a family member? Discuss what happened and how it was resolved.

9. Identify several examples in the story of ways that the Depression affected lower- and middle-class people.

10. Compare and contrast the personalities of Dessie and Lem.
   a. In what ways are they similar? In what ways are they different?
   b. Which character are you most like? Why?

11. Characters often evolve or change in a story. In this story, our view of Pap's past changes.
   a. Discuss how your ideas about Pap changed throughout the story.
   b. Have you ever been misunderstood before? How did this affect you?
   c. Have you ever thought something about someone only to find out later that you were completely wrong? What did you do about this? How did it affect you?

12. Create an alternate ending for the story describing what would have happened to the Soames family if Miz Emily had not forgiven Mam.

13. When you love or care for others, you often make sacrifices for them.
   a. Give examples of characters in the story making sacrifices for others.
   b. Have you ever made a sacrifice for someone you care about? Explain.
   c. Has someone ever made a sacrifice for you? Explain.

14. Discuss whether you think Dessie made a good choice or a bad choice in taking Lem to Lexington to find Davy Shaw.
   a. Have you ever taken a risk that changed your life? If so, how do you feel about your decision?
   b. Have you ever made a bad choice? What happened and how was it resolved?

15. At the end of the story, Dessie believes her father's spirit helped guide the Soames' to their new life at the family horse farm. Do you agree or disagree? Do you think it was Dessie's destiny to leave Whitburn and go to Lexington? After all, her name is Destiny Rose. Answer the following:
    a. What is destiny?
    b. Can you control it or is it already set?
    c. What do you believe to be your destiny?
    d. What role does your family have in helping you fulfill your destiny?

A Classroom Teaching Guide by Megan Durham for Blue Dust Days is available for purchase as an e-book at http://www.hearttoheartpublishinginc.com